ARKS OF AMERICA

The Arks Chronicles, Book One

D.A. CAREY

D.A. CAREY

Part One

AN IDEA

"The world is a dangerous place to live, not because of the people who are evil, but because of the people who don't do anything about it."

- Albert Einstein

"As Denver enters the twelfth day of the sanitation strike, commerce and travel in the city are being ground to a halt. Striking sanitation workers, along with sympathetic parties from other unions, have virtually stopped access to many businesses in the metro area. Workers trying to cross the lines to go to office buildings have been pelted with rocks and bottles. Police spokespeople advise they are too undermanned to stop the protests and are unable to locate the individuals responsible for the attacks. A representative from the mayor's office stated they are negotiating with sanitation workers but are at a fiscal impasse. They say there is not enough money in the budget to hire more workers to accommodate ten weeks paid time off for each worker as they demand. The twenty-five percent pay increase would make each sanitation worker's average salary with benefits worth over $150,000 annually. A fiscal outlay of this magnitude would either mean cuts to school funding or increased taxes. State law does not allow for more tax increases for two years.

"In related news, there are reports of both city water and sanitation service interruptions. It's unclear if those outages are related to the sympathetic strikes of other city unions. They could be common service failures to the city's antiquated utilities system or an act of sabotage.

"City officials are still investigating. As of yet, no one has claimed responsibility."

. . .

Susan Willis was trying to hold back tears as she spoke to her boss at Cavanaugh Corp. "Mr. Clark, I'm sorry, I won't be able to make it in today."

"I understand, Susan. Is everything okay?"

"Yes and no. I'm so sorry. I know I was supposed to help with the presentation Mr. Cavanaugh is doing today. I tried, I really did," Susan poured out in a rush. "Everywhere I turned there were striking workers and riots. I tried to get around, and they threw things at my car and broke my windows."

"Are you okay? Is there anything I can do?" Louis asked.

"I think I'm okay. The policeman took my report, and an EMT bandaged my face. All I want to do now is go home. I'm so sorry."

"Susan, you need to focus on taking care of yourself. We're fine here. If there is anything I can do, please let me know. Take the rest of the week off and don't worry about using your PTO. You've been through a lot."

DAVE

"Chaos, destruction, and division are instruments and the calling card of evil. Order, community, and cooperation are the embodiment of good," Dave said aloud, pausing to look over the panorama of beauty. He was lost in thought, unaware if the silent companion behind him noticed or heard.

Dave Cavanaugh was a thinker and a planner. In a different era, he might have been called a philosopher. This hike was to remind himself why he felt so driven to do this thing. Things that should be simple and obvious, many people tried to make more complex.

To a casual observer, Dave resembled a weather-worn hiker in his fifties. Few would guess he was closer to seventy. Tanned from years in the sun and a shade over six feet tall, he still had most of his hair, although it was a silvery gray now with only a hint of the sandy blond it had once been. He was lean and trim, with the wiry muscles of a hiker and outdoorsman, not the bulk of a body built in the gym. At his age, he was proud he still had the strength to climb mountains.

The view from this vantage point was breathtaking. Dave sat on the side of a mountain overlooking the valley of South Park, Colorado. He could see the town of Fairplay in the distance. The cattle herds that dotted the plains of the valley were only small moving dots from this distance. He reveled in the unspoiled beauty of the valley. This area always reminded him of an old B-grade movie he remembered from the seventies about someone's vision of Shangri-La. It didn't look the same; it just felt the way Dave imagined it would. To him, this *was* Shangri-La. The mountains circling the valley protected it from the worst of people and elements in a timeless way much as he imagined Shangri-La might have in that mythical valley.

Mt. Sherman and Horseshoe Mountain rose in the distance, and nearer to him were woods, streams, pines, and sycamore trees. Dave never understood why more people didn't come to this valley. Then again, it probably would have ruined it if they did. The air was crisp, and the clouds crowned the ring of mountains surrounding the huge valley. The towns below hadn't changed much in the last hundred years. The old western feel of a small town that supported cattle ranches and silver mines across the west remained. The roads were mostly paved in town now. Some buildings were still made of wood, others brick or stone.

The cattle herds were still there. At this time of year, they probably had newly born calves, still gawky and playful like a twelve-year-old boy. They could have been descendants of cattle herds driven into the valley more than a hundred years earlier.

Dave let out a sigh of contentment. The feel of the high mountain air in his lungs made him feel younger, more invigorated, and complete. At this stage in his life, he pondered that although change was inevitable, bringing construction to this valley was akin to desecration of a sacred site.

When being honest with himself, he had to admit that this valley didn't exactly fit his model for the aggressive new phase of his business. Yet his mind and desire kept being drawn back here. He could allow a bit of vanity to enter into this one part of the business venture. This was a place he came to before he made his wealth. He hoped to be here at the end of his journey as well.

In a way, Dave saw these towns as freeholds that he envisioned as part biblical ark and part old western fort.

He turned to Levi, as he found himself doing more often of late. Levi didn't try to offer much in the way of business advice and didn't try to persuade or dissuade. Although many years younger, he was turning into a good friend that enjoyed the solitude of the mountains as much as Dave and was a solid sounding board. Levi knew when to talk and when to listen. That was a rare skill set.

Levi stood nearly six foot four, with massive shoulders and dark hair. Although his stature may have been atypical of his Jewish heritage, aside from his height and bulk, his face, hair, and general features fit in so well with a family line that could trace his culture back hundreds of years on both sides of his family.

Still looking out over the valley, Dave mused. "Levi, would you consider yourself a student of history?"

"Yes sir, but my people have a different view of history than many Christians, or even the average American. While I was born in the U.S., as was my mother, my father and all my grandparents are either from Europe, or more specifically Germany, before the war."

Dave was deep in thought, turning over things in his mind. Levi knew him well enough not to press the conversation. While any student of history knows that no nation stands forever, very few people stopped to think about the other important factors in that equation. Dave viewed a nation or corporation like a person. All entities go through childhood, puberty, then on to maturity, and eventually old age and death. Each nation, corporation, sports team, or any entity went through the same stages, even if the era of that life span and the appearance and feel of the stages were different. While one nation might go through that cycle in a millennium, another might go through the same cycle in a scant two hundred years. The trick was to be able to accurately and dispassionately see and understand the signs of where a business venture or nation might be in a life cycle and not apply a human lifespan to that thought process. Sometimes the change from stage to stage wasn't violent or even that noticeable. In any given year, a college basketball team could return many of the same players from a previous year. That team could mature into a great last second team or a great decision-making team this year when they had not been previously. The instinctive knowledge to see and predict those changes helped Dave be ahead of the curve in industry trends, contract negotiations, and strategic plans.

That was the secret to Dave's success. In addition to providing an excellent service at a good rate on a scale few others could, Dave knew people, companies, teams, and nations. He knew them instinctively on a level few others did. It was that knowledge and skillset that had Dave so convinced he was right in his current and most audacious plan. This would be his biggest venture yet and maybe one of the most important in this country's history if he was right.

The knowledge that change was coming was growing in popularity, not only in the U.S., but in other countries as well. Dave believed it too and was convinced he was the right man at the right time to make a difference.

There would be profit to be made as well. There was nothing unethical in providing people with goods or services they wanted at a reasonable price. That was the system America was founded on. The ace in the hole that Dave thought he had was time. Most people had a hard time wrapping their minds around the lifespan of a country. He was convinced this country was in the stage of old age, with corruption eating at its bones like a cancer. The symptoms were many, and that meant the things that could bring down an old and brittle body were many more than when the country was young and healthy. Things like race riots, natural disasters, infrastructure failures, wars, EMP strikes, terrorism, or even political plots from within were just a few.

It was frustrating to know that the country should have been able to last for a thousand years. Like an alcoholic, Americans had abused and overindulged to the point where their national lifespan was shorter than it should have been. Now, after two hundred and fifty years, the country was old and brittle beyond its years and susceptible to all manner of maladies. The trick of time for a nation was that while any malady might befall the country today or tomorrow, it might also totter on for another fifty to a hundred years as well.

"Levi, my friend," Dave said after rousing himself from his reverie, "I'll admit my heart is heavy. The village we have planned up here will be unobtrusive and fit in with nature and this valley in every way possible. Yet, at the same time, I'll always feel like I'm spoiling this place. I have reconciled myself and am quite comfortable with the business side of this venture. I've no doubts about its ethics and profitability. In addition to the homes and village, it will be like a mutual fund that focuses on the kinds of goods that have more value after a global catastrophe. In some instances, we will own parts of the company, and in others, we will own the entire company. When possible, we will move those factories near one of our charter towns, except for here. I will not bring industry to this valley. We'll use some of the old silver mines I bought up here to expand into massive warehouses of goods both for ourselves and our other towns."

"Mr. Cavanaugh, your judgment has always been sound. This business will make money, you know that. You've said you see these towns as gated cities for people with shared values, like a lifeboat prepared for an event that brings the nation to its knees. All of that makes sense to me, and it will to a lot of people who follow you as well. If this location is giving you heartburn, then limit the guest list here to people you genuinely like and who will love this valley the way you do. There will be plenty of other charter towns to go around."

"Thank you, Levi. Once again, you've helped me work through my thoughts and settle this in my mind. Let's stop the shop talk and have a bite to eat before we make the hike back. What's for lunch?"

"Let me guess, you have a couple of Kind bars, some beef jerky, and some trail mix in your pack," Levi teased.

"Am I that predictable?"

"Only in some things." Levi pulled both an apple and an orange from his pack. He cut into the apple with an Israeli Special Forces knife. Dave knew the knife was an Ari B' Lilah, not something you could simply walk in to a store and buy. In Levi's hands, it resembled a paring knife going through the apple, yet Dave wondered what else that knife had seen or gone through in years past. Levi didn't talk much about his war experiences. Dave respected that and didn't press. As close and he and Levi had become, he sometimes envied the way Levi and his own nephew

Vince could share things they wouldn't with anyone else. They shared a mutual bond the way only two warriors could who had seen and shared some of the same terrors.

The men finished their food in silence, enjoying the mountain. They put their garbage back in their packs to carry out in order to preserve the beauty and purity of the mountain. With a nod, Dave started hiking. Levi followed like a huge mountain cat following his prey like a shadow, silent, deadly, and protective.

"Mr. Cavanaugh, I received a communication a moment ago directing us to divert the chopper to Colorado Springs when we leave. The corporate leadership team has suggested a temporary move of key personnel from the corporate office in Denver to the backup facility in Colorado Springs," Levi said after reading a message on his satellite connected device.

Pausing on the narrow dirt path, Dave turned. "Really? What's going on?"

"Apparently the sanitation workers' strike in Denver has expanded. They're blocking roads and access to businesses by claiming that anyone who goes to work is a scab crossing their lines. There has been violence as well."

"Idiots."

"Furthermore, we're getting reports of sympathetic strikes and work stoppages by the water and sewage utility workers. Those are creating work and travel interruptions as well. The communication says they have advised most workers to telecommute and some key personnel to come to the Colorado Springs remote location for a week or two."

"Okay. Please make sure they know I want that option extended to their families as well. We will, of course, reimburse hotel or apartment rental for those who need to leave their homes," Dave said, his whole posture switching into full CEO mode.

VINCE

The gravel crunched under Vince's tires as he rolled into the place where he planned to meet Greg for hunting a few minutes ahead of schedule.

The dogs were restless in the carrier in the back of the truck. It was nice to relax for a few moments and take it all in. He was reveling in the quietness of a chilly December morning in Kentucky. He loved the country here. It was comfortable, like the way a man who knows his house can walk through it in total darkness because he knows every corner and piece of furniture. Vince loved this time of year with the crisp breezes that promised a threat of real cold. The crunch of the frosty grass and the gurgle of the narrow creeks that hadn't yet frozen created a visceral sensation and memory that stayed with him much like the perfume of his wife or the smell of his grandmother's kitchen when she baked. This resonated with some men in their soul in a way that was hard to put in plain words but brought a sense of contentment and "rightness."

Sitting here contemplating this reminded Vince of the feeling of comfort and joy he used to experience in seeing the silhouette of his wife or daughter walking in the distance. He knew their shape and movement with only the briefest glance. It didn't matter if he could only see their shadow with the sun behind them. He couldn't explain why or how, he just knew his home and family the way a wolf knew his pack.

Vince was a strong man and wide through the shoulders, with piercing blue eyes that ran somewhere a shade between ice and ocean water and could bore right through a man. He was about six feet tall and had recently put on a bit of weight around the waist he needed to work on. His hair was a sandy blond color that he liked to say was a lighter color of mud. He kept it short and trimmed. His father's family was from the Rocky Mountains in Colorado. By the time Vince was born, they'd moved to the suburbs of Denver. His family in Colorado hiked and owned a cabin in the mountains. They loved and communed with nature; that was fulfilling and yet different than he was doing now. The Colorado branch of the family even boasted a billionaire outdoorsman, Vince's uncle Dave.

It wasn't until Vince's parents divorced and his mother moved back to Kentucky and eventually remarried that Vince learned to truly enjoy the outdoors this way. It wasn't that he hadn't enjoyed it before; his family appreciated the beauty of the Colorado mountains that many people never would. It was after finally getting to know, respect, and love his stepfather that Vince saw nature in a different way and understood life and nature so much better. The circle of life and the delicate balance of nature, forests, and animals were impressive and delicate when truly experienced and understood. Man could play a role in destroying this balance or strengthening it if he participated with knowledge and respect. It was important to know which trees were which, which roots were edible, and how to find water or dig a well.

Vince didn't immediately take to the woods with his stepfather. He rebelled and snuck out at night to run the streets. He smoked, drank, and got into more than his fair share of trouble. Eventually his stepfather, Dan, won him over. Not by trying to be his dad, but by being a friend and mentor. They spent a lot of time working outdoors and hunting. Although Vince didn't know it at the time, he was learning to be a man and have a traditional man's value system and some self-sufficiency skills.

Later, Vince moved away, travelled, and eventually joined the Army. He did a couple of tours in Iraq and Afghanistan. He always believed it was the life skills Dan taught him that helped keep him alive. At a minimum, it was this mindset that helped keep him centered emotionally when many didn't have the mental place of security or faith to fall back on.

Even with those skills, the years at the end of his Army career and the beginning of his marriage passed in a blur. The last tour in Afghanistan was harder. There didn't appear to be a clear mission. Many of the locals didn't want them there. The "esprit de corps" or clarity of mission wasn't what it had been in the beginning. Either that or Vince was getting older and more jaded. It was hard to go on patrol and see a friend get injured, maimed, or killed and struggle with what they had accomplished or what good they were doing. It was during that time that Vince met a man who would later become his best friend.

Levi Goldman and Vince met during a series of joint operations between the

Israeli and American Special Forces units. Levi and Vince spent a lot of time talking over drinks when off duty. In the field, they instinctively knew what the other would do or need. It was Levi who talked at length about the history of the Jewish people and the enemies they'd faced over the centuries. Knowing they couldn't make everyone like them or even respect them, sometimes all they could do was choose the ground on which they fought and which units they sent into battle, or more importantly, which issues were worth fighting for.

"If nothing is worth fighting for, then that means we hold nothing of higher value than another thing," Levi reasoned.

Levi's immediate family wasn't from Israel; they were from New York. The events of 9/11 hit close to home for him. There was nothing surprising to Levi about a terrorist attack. What was most tragic to him was that for that one day and for that battle, the conflict was fought in our country and in our cities. "Their fighters against our civilians," Levi explained.

Vince remembered the conversation as clear as if it were yesterday. They were in a remote part of Afghanistan. Vince was further in his Army career and not too many months away from leaving service. When a soldier started struggling with the "why" of what they were doing, it was a good sign to change professions.

It was during that time that Levi counseled: "Vince, my friend, do you doubt that this part of the world raises and grooms terrorists much the same way people in Kansas raise wheat?"

"I know that's true," Vince countered wryly. "It still bothers me. How do we know that these missions or patrols are doing any good?"

"We don't. You of all people know that in all the things we have to do our job, our piece of the puzzle. It's a job we are trained for. We know we have to trust the man beside us to do his part while we do ours. We need and trust commanders to make good strategic decisions. We don't have the time or luxury to second guess them. Just as you can't be checking to see if my rifle is loaded, my gear is straight, and I've got my sector covered during a firefight. That's my job."

"That's all true."

"Vince, I'll say one more word on the subject then we put this to bed, okay?" Levi spoke with the hint of an Israeli accent that came out when he was passionate about something. He'd picked up the accent more from his comrades in the Israeli army than his upbringing in New York. "Never forget that people like you and I are volunteers. We are well trained and know the risks and why we are here. We are fighting the terrorists and despots in their home territory, not ours. At a minimum, we are keeping them busy. At best, we've killed a threat that may have been planning a trip to yours or my home town in America. Every logic train or stream of thought should begin with that. For this topic, I choose to begin my thoughts or reasoning with *faith* in the belief that fighting them here saves lives at home."

Vince got out of the Army and came back home to the world. He got married, got a job, and became a father to the most beautiful baby girl in the world. He focused on trying to live life and stay in the struggle to move up and ahead in life and work. They worked to buy a home, take vacations, and do the things most Americans did.

All that didn't leave Vince much time in the woods. Although he missed it, there was a feeling that there wasn't time and a fear that if he fell back in love with that lifestyle he couldn't put his all into climbing the corporate ladder. The cubicles and corporate politics didn't have the same importance or sense of urgency in comparison. Vince wasn't one to hide his feelings well. He had to focus and direct all his energies to being successful in his job. So Vince dove deep into the corporate lifestyle and worked, travelled, drank, played golf, and boated, like many other people.

He fit right in and was good at it. Good at the work he did, good at golf, and good at boating, drinking, and carousing, which made him bad at marriage. If people were honest and without emotion after a divorce, they could acknowledge that there was blame enough to go around. When Vince was honest with himself, he could admit that most of the blame was his. There were some things he wished his wife would have done differently, yet in his heart, he knew that if he had been the husband he should have been, he'd still be married and being the dad he wanted to be to his daughter.

It was during the rocky portion of his marriage leading up to his divorce that Vince started spending more time with his stepfather Dan. As was Dan's way, he didn't give advice unless directly asked. He didn't lecture; he just smiled and lived and enjoyed each moment as if it was his last. And he taught. Dan was always teaching something. It was in spending that time with Dan on his farm, in the woods, and with his dogs hunting that Vince finally started to feel centered again. He hadn't realized he'd lost his center until he rediscovered it. By that time, the damage was done. Too many harsh things had been said and done. Divorce was the result.

Vince was never a very extroverted type with his emotions or deepest feelings. When things got bad, Vince got quiet or diverted his emotions elsewhere. So as work had its own stresses and the divorce and lawyers and court dates worked through their painful process, Vince spent more time with Dan in the woods or stopping by country diners for lunch and laughs with the local old timers. It kept him sane. The process of going through a divorce was bad. The guilt that it created for him with his now ex-wife and daughter took its toll.

They say that out of adversity there is a silver lining to the cloud if we keep an eye out for it. This period served as a wakeup call and a catalyst to get Vince back to who he should be. His only regret was that he hadn't got there sooner.

Then out of the blue, Dan announced he had cancer and only a short time to live.

It was unthinkable and devastating to believe that Dan could be dying. He was such a strong and vigorous man. They'd hunted the previous weekend. Over the two days, he probably walked twenty-five miles. Dan appeared so healthy, in his early sixties and still a strong man by most accounts.

In Dan's way, he handled it stoically and with a smile and actually made the people that came to weep with him laugh with him instead. They left him with a smile on their face and a tear in their eyes.

Dan fought the cancer hard and turned the month they gave him into a year, then into eighteen months, but the disease was too strong and Dan succumbed.

On the day of his funeral, the small church in the country that was older than the state was inundated by hundreds and possibly over a thousand people who came to pay their respects. Dan was one of the most well-liked and respected men in the community. Eventually the condolences, food, and well-wishers waned, and Vince's mother was left alone on the farm with the horses, dogs, and chickens, and a huge hole in her heart and soul.

It was around this time that Vince's ex-wife Ellie announced she and Kate were moving to Chicago where Ellie would pursue a new job. The move would allow Kate to attend college and eventually law school where she always wanted.

Vince was left with a big, empty house meant for a family, not a single man. The job he did by day sometimes felt like an endless ladder to nowhere. He had the hunting dogs and horses left to him in Dan's will but no best friend to hunt or do things with. It was the type of low point that could drive many men to drink. It wasn't that Vince was against drinking, it was that he'd done so much of it when he was younger and seen it do so much damage to friends and family that at an early age he taught himself a sort of alcohol defense mechanism. Vince only drank when things were good, when a hard day of work was done, a promotion gained, or in celebration of a wedding or birthday. When things in life were hard, when work was a struggle, or when there was an argument at home, he didn't drink. Partly from habit, though mostly because he might not be able to crawl out of it later.

It was one of Dan's best friends and hunting buddies, Greg, in particular that got him back out hunting again and living life with the smile that Dan taught him. Unfortunately, there were fewer and fewer places to hunt. Dan had known everyone in the county and was friends with them, not Vince. The family farm as a way of life was dying, and that made it harder still.

When Vince got back in his truck, the radio program he caught midway through was discussing recent attacks on police and rehashing or debating an older case in which several policemen were shot in Dallas a few years ago:

"...that case it was an individual who was part of a domestic hate group that attacked policemen in Dallas. The problem with that case, which many of us brought up at the time, is that it was the first one to legitimize attacks on police."

"Wow, that's a strong statement. Nothing legitimizes attacks or gun violence. I don't know if I'd go that far."

"Wait a moment, if you remember, at the time there was no immediate outcry from the president and other leaders decrying the attack. In fact, the country's top law enforcement leader, the U.S. attorney general, released statements sympathetic to the attackers and their organization."

"I remember the president came out with some strong language condemning the attacks."

"Yes, but that wasn't until sometime later. It was easy to tell it was prompted by the national criticism of his initial tepid response to the attacks. By that time the damage was done, policemen knew they weren't supported, if they didn't know it before. More importantly, these radical domestic organizations were emboldened to plan more attacks because their terrorist type strategies were not condemned. Although it is my opinion that they were supported at the top levels of government."

"To say it was supported may be a strong statement. Perhaps I would agree to say they weren't condemned strongly enough."

"Okay, then we are down to semantics at that point. You have to remember that the Dallas police shootings didn't come long after the mayor in Baltimore encouraged rioting and police shootings in her own city. It wasn't long after those events that the president sent the attorney general to Missouri to investigate police there."

"Are you saying that the president should not have sent the attorney general to Missouri?"

"Yes and no. The American people have to know the president is in tune with their needs and will use all the tools at his or her disposal for both the good of the country and the individual. From that view, I understand the desire for some type of involvement from the executive branch. However, I don't believe the president had any personal experience with racism of that sort and was not responding out of a connection to the event, but was rather pandering to a voting bloc."

"True, he is a politician. We all know that. This is not a discussion on that president's accomplishments or failures and—"

"You're right, however, we can't discuss the police shootings and general decline in our police work and rise in crime over the past decade without looking at events like Dallas, Baltimore, and the president's response in a cause and effect way."

"Okay, I'll bite. How do you think those events directly impacted where we are today?"

"It's simple and direct. First, a president who was powerful and popular in many areas chose to exert his response or non-response to affect some of these internal radical organizations and their approach. I believe strongly that the facts support that his actions confirmed this radical course of action for those groups. Second, you have the events in Baltimore, New York, Texas, and Missouri that put policemen on notice that, despite some election time rhetoric, they don't have the support of their leadership at the highest levels. If they do something difficult or confrontational, there is a very good chance they will be fired or prosecuted. These men and women don't make enough money to justify that risk, so many of the best and brightest are leaving this noble calling. Some of the replacements are not as well trained or noble in their approach. I fully acknowledge that we have always had sporadic cases of corrupt policemen or horrendous wrongs that need to be righted, as happened in North Carolina. It's important that we treat those as exceptions and not the rule or an excuse for domestic terrorism."

"Thank you. After a short break to pay our sponsors, we will return with the market report..."

ELLIE

Kate bounded down the wooden stairs of the old three-story home in Chicago's northwest side. "Mom, this is so cool!"

"What's so cool, hun?" Ellie responded with an amused smile. It did her heart good to see her daughter so exuberant and happy. In truth, Kate and Vince were alike in more ways than either of them noticed. She worried about Kate missing home and time with her dad.

Kate beamed. "I can see the tops of the tall buildings in downtown Chicago from my bedroom, and there's a subway station only three blocks from here! I can finally do things my friends back home only talk about. I can go to Navy Pier or get really good pizza or anything else I want." Kate's unrestrained tone reminded Ellie more of the child she had been and less of the more cynical teenager she acted like sometimes.

"Well, you need to be careful, young lady. You didn't grow up here, and this isn't Kentucky. Bad things can happen," Ellie cautioned.

"Mom, you worry all the time. You're starting to sound like Dad."

"L-o-l," Elli said, mimicking the textspeak Kate used so often. "Okay, I'll stop. I don't want to be that obsessed about all the bad things that can happen."

"He didn't even get excited when I got into the University of Chicago," Kate said in a dejected tone. Kate didn't normally open up often and share her inner feelings, so Ellie knew this was important to her. "Mom, that was my dream, and he barely sounded excited. He has no idea what a special school this is and how much it means to me."

"Honey, your dad worries so much about you because he loves you. He probably worries more now than ever." Ellie pulled Kate in for a hug. "I'm sure he'll miss you so much more than you can know. It's hard to show excitement when you have those feelings underneath."

"Well, *you're* excited for me," she whined.

Ellie smiled. "Yes, but I'm here with you. I get to see you every day."

"Aren't you excited to be here? It's like you can do everything here and you couldn't do anything in Kentucky."

"Honey, I'll always miss Kentucky. It was home to me for so long. It has family and friends and so much good to offer. You'll miss it in time, too. Honestly, I already do some," Ellie said wistfully. "Yet this is a fresh start," she continued. "I love Malcolm, and he's a good man. This will be a great school and experience for you as well. It's the right thing at the right time for both of us. And *yes*, I'm excited too! I love shopping here and all the restaurants. The pace of life is vastly different than Kentucky."

Ellie watched Kate skip out of the house and noted with pride that she could make being dressed simply appear so trendy. She was wearing skinny jeans and a chic top from one of the expensive stores. Her hair was in a ponytail. She used to wear it that way all the time for comfort and because her dad liked it. These days she wore it that way less often, instead choosing to go a little bit more stylish and adult with her hair and makeup. Additionally, Kate wore the Nike shoes she insisted her dad buy her where they put her name on the side. Kate would never be the tall, long-legged runway model. She was close to five feet tall, trim and cute with strawberry blonde hair and her father's piercing blue eyes. She was what some would call more of a "Maryanne" than a "Ginger," despite the red tints in her hair. Being full of energy and focus and incredibly smart, older people would see something in Kate and insist she was an old soul.

Kate's friend from high school in Kentucky was also going to U. Chicago, which made the transition easier. During the visits up here and introductions to Malcolm, Kate had already made an impressive circle of friends. While Ellie was proud of Kate, it was a bit melancholy, knowing these new beginnings confirmed that a part of her life in Kentucky and with Vince was definitely over. She'd left her life, home, and friends in Kentucky behind to start anew here.

Now it was only a matter of time before Kate moved out and on with her life and spent less time at home. It gave Ellie an insight into how Vince must be feeling. Ellie knew in her heart that the divorce was the right thing and she had to move on. Still, she could admit to herself that she cared for him. She just couldn't live with him.

Part Two

PLANNING AND PREPPING

"When there is no vision, there is no hope."

-George Washington Carver

DAVE

Dave began drawing on the plastic-covered map and making notes on the adjacent whiteboard.

He and Levi were alone in the large main room of the cabin on the side of a mountain on the edge of the South Park valley. Dave needed this time to collect and organize his thoughts in seclusion. Louis was the only other one who joined these sessions. Early in his career, Dave enjoyed these times alone and allowed no one else to join. He found that he now preferred the companionship and sounding board of Levi, and Louis' loyalty and efficiency.

In the early days, Dave used a very small cabin lower in the South Park valley he built himself on a small parcel of land. As much as he missed the cozy spot, it wasn't practical anymore. Now they used the huge resort-style cabin that was built on the side of a mountain with a commanding view.

As was his custom once a decision was made, it was full steam ahead. Dave preferred to get his thoughts in order here at the cabin before going back to meet with the suits in Denver. He already owned a large tract of land near the mountain on the edge of the valley that was enough to do what he needed.

Purchase options on any adjacent land that might be coming available, he wrote on the whiteboard.

"How do options help?" Levi asked.

"Not much immediately. However, by paying the local owners a fee, it allows us first choice to purchase their land at a fair price if they do decide to sell. I like it because ethically it tells them I *do* want to purchase land in the area adjacent to what I already own on their timeframe with no pressure. I'm not trying to do anything underhanded. If they choose to sell, then I'd like first shot is all."

Research old abandoned mine ownership adjacent to our property and the lake. Purchase any that can be had, he added to the whiteboard.

"Dave, won't all these land purchases cause a stir in the valley?"

"Yes," Dave agreed with a snort, pausing to smile over his shoulder. "Part of the value of being the local eccentric billionaire is that people tend to shrug off things like this most of the time."

Dave quit writing and sat down. "I've been turning over a few ideas for how to structure this new company. I have some ideas about the land ownership I want to run by the attorneys at corporate. I'm not sure how to put it all in words yet. We need to settle on the best solution for how to title the land and set up the corporation and community bylaws fairly quickly.

Chuckling, he mused, "For what I'm paying them and how many of them there are, if they can't solve this, I should fire the whole passel of them."

He took a drink and stood back up to make more notes on the whiteboard. "Levi, you sure you don't mind taking these notes? It's not your job. I have a whole staff of eager interns who wonder why they aren't allowed to do more of this. They're chomping at the bit to spend more time on strategic things with the leadership team. As far as anyone knows, you're only here to be my bodyguard. Later when this takes off, we'll announce you as the head of security for the entire project."

"Well, boss, despite my outward appearance, I *do* have a college education, and my mother would be proud to see me putting it to use. Besides, it's easier to keep you safe when it's only me and you in the room. I have to admit that when you're using me as a sounding board, I'm learning more. I like getting to see how your mind works." Levi grinned. "Besides, you have no idea how many people would pay for this level of access to Dave Cavanaugh, the Richard Branson of the Rockies!"

"Young man, why I oughta..." Dave threw a dry erase marker at him.

After a snort, he turned right back to his work. He was like that. His mind was so nimble he could change gears from one topic to another in the blink of an eye and be totally absorbed in the next topic before you knew it. Levi understood that, as his mother was the same way.

Dave made special instructions for the architects and planners as to how he wanted to build this village, or charter town, in such a way as to make it both secure and have the design blend in with the nature and beauty of this valley. It was important to make it as unobtrusive as possible.

Levi continued taking notes, careful not to interrupt much when Dave was deep into the creative thought process. Dave was not rude or domineering like many men with his wealth, power, and position would be. He was kind and understanding, like you would expect of a favorite uncle. It was hard not to hold Dave in a little bit of awe or be disappointed in yourself if you derailed his thoughts. No one wanted to disappoint Dave Cavanaugh. He was the type of man who brought out the best in those around him.

While Dave wasn't curing cancer, he *was* coming up with some rather interesting and profitable ideas that could save a lot of lives and knowledge. His ideas had a simplicity to them that in retrospect left people to wonder why no one else had done it.

Dave was interrupted, though, and not by Levi. His thoughts were interrupted by a discomfort pressing against his hip. "Levi, this thing is a pain. I don't think I'll ever get used to carrying a gun."

"I know you hate the necessity, boss. I hate it for you, but the world is changing, and it's good for you to have this and know how to use it."

Levi had helped him choose from a few that he carried at different times to get used to. He had been given more than enough by friends once they noticed him carrying. The Coonan .357 compact fit snug on his hip in a soft, hand-tooled leather holster. Although he doubted anything would happen here in these mountains, he needed to get used to carrying it and make it a habit.

"You'll get used to it, boss."

"I hope so, and I hope not. Knowing I need it isn't the same as liking it."

"I understand, but you have to stop thinking of it like a gun or a symbol of destruction. It's merely a tool. Each tool is a good or evil as the person holding it," Levi said earnestly.

"I know you're right," Dave responded without much conviction.

"Mr. Cavanaugh," Levi only used his last name when he had something important to say, "as you've said yourself, times are changing. This country is not what it was fifty or a hundred years ago. Heck, you're betting billions of your own and other people's money on the fact that things are going downhill. I know you've said it probably won't get bad in your lifetime, and possibly not in mine, but it *will* get bad sometime. There is one thing I know well, and perhaps on this one thing I know more than you. Do you know what that one thing is?"

"Tell me." Dave turned his full attention on Levi.

"What I know is bad people will have guns no matter what. They will use them as a tool to plunder, rape, and kill. If good men like you don't carry guns and impose their will in the name of justice, then who stands between you and those bad men?"

"What about you, Levi? You and men like my nephew? You're good men."

"No sir, you still don't get it." Levi's face betrayed his frustration at not being able to explain himself the way he wanted. “Men like me are merely tools, a means to accomplish a goal. We’re no different than that gun on your hip. The difference between me and other men like me is that I harbor no illusions about who or what I am. I don’t want to be part of evil, so I worked hard to be aligned with good people. I count myself lucky to work for you.”

“And my nephew?”

“He is a rare one,” Levi said with a smile that showed pride in his best friend. “Right now, he’s a tool like me. His only problem is that his conscience and mind work a lot harder on him. He keeps reliving what he’s done and been forced to do as a man and as a soldier. He can’t see or accept that the ruthless things he’s done are not his fault. He could no more walk away from a fight or refuse to defend someone weak or in need than I could stop breathing.”

Dave chuckled. “That doesn’t sound so much different from the Levi I know, except for the brooding.”

“Maybe not,” Levi acquiesced. “But what he does have is the ability to be good and noble on a higher level like you. That’s different and beyond me. That’s a nobility of spirit few men have. That’s why other men follow him. He doesn’t even know he has it buried in him. He would be angry or embarrassed if he heard me say it. Yet it’s still true. Even though he’s not the empire builder you are, he is a leader that men will lay down their lives for.”

“Thank you, Levi. It does my heart good to hear you speak that way of my nephew. I also think you sell yourself short, although that’s a topic for another time. On another topic, I’ve wanted to ask about your family back in New York. Do you need to go home and help?”

“No, they’re fine. I don’t know if I told you about my cousin who is one of New York’s finest. It was his partner that was shot in the incident covered in the news last week.”

“That’s terrible. Was your cousin hurt?”

“He’s fine. He was off that day for a family event so he’s carrying a lot of guilt right now, thinking he might have been able to help.”

“I know there are riots in the city and crime rates are soaring. What did your family say about that?”

“To them it’s more of a tragic chain of events that’s so wasteful and they can’t find a way out of. The riots and the police shootings prompted the chief of police to go back to two officers per car and change the patrol schedule to cover each other’s back better. That means the NYPD can be in fewer places at a time, giving the criminals and rioters more confidence to spread their crime spree and chaos.”

“These things make me feel impotent,” Dave said, exasperated. “Don’t our leaders know that this genie will not be put back in the bottle as easy as it was let out?" Dave held up his hand. "You don't have to answer; I'm just ranting. Did Louis tell you what happened to one of the women on his staff here in Denver the other day?"

"Yes, thank God she wasn't hurt badly."

"That's true, yet I don't know how much longer we can count on those small saving graces. Things always escalate bit by bit unless something drastic happens to change events. You've seen what's going on in Denver and other cities. You've talked to your family in New York. What will happen next? Things always escalate."

While they waited for the chopper to take them back to Denver, Levi handed Dave a tablet with a satellite download of the intelligence assessment related to the civil unrest in Denver:

"City, state, and federal officials appear to be making ground in the negotiations with Denver sanitation union officials. While the strike is not over, the fact that officials are meeting and talking is a good sign. In other news, the investigation into the water and sewage outages still has not determined if they are failures of age or sabotage. Considering the timing and widespread impacts, most experts agree that sabotage is the more likely cause.

"The impact to the city in relation to the federal response to the riots and strikes has emboldened unions in cities like San Francisco, Chicago, and New York to threaten similar strikes. Those unions are getting a lot of push from members who also belong to radical domestic organizations that favor a more drastic or terroristic-type approach to domestic change..."

LIZ

Sitting at the makeup stand getting ready for another Hollywood gala to promote or support something or other, Liz had already lost track of what this one was for.

The events could be so tedious. Her wealth and success were still somewhat new to her. The home she now lived in was more opulent than anything she lived in growing up. The huge master bedroom and dressing area alone was more like an extravagant hotel than her home.

"Carol," Liz called into the other room. "What's this thing tonight all about anyway? I know you told me. I think sometimes I tune out the things I don't want to do. I'm sorry."

"Liz!" Carol chided. "It's only the biggest event of the season. It's an award ceremony that raises money to protect endangered species in addition to celebrating achievement in entertainment."

"I like that." Liz nodded. "What endangered species are they protecting and where?"

"I don't think that's important," Carol said. "The important part is that the red carpet photos will be in all the major magazines and on all television networks. It's a wonderful chance for you to be seen at your best, dazzling for the cameras."

Liz was working hard to stifle a giggle, "Don't they have photos of me looking *simply my best* at all the previous awards ceremonies? Can't they just rerun those and we could stay home and eat ice cream and watch it on TV?"

"Honestly, Liz!" Carol said in exasperation. "This is important. You have to keep your public views and internet searches high to command the best roles and contracts. This is a perfect event for that."

"I suppose," Liz reluctantly admitted. "Still, I actually do care about the endangered species. Doesn't anyone else care about them?" Liz giggled.

"No, not in this town, Liz," Carol said matter-of-factly. "It's career suicide not to have a cause and prove your acting chops by pushing that agenda very publicly and sincerely. However, it's naïve and silly to actually care behind closed doors. I know it sounds disingenuous, but that's how the game is played."

Liz was a beautiful actress who was rapidly becoming known worldwide. She had burst onto the scene with a few movies that were very successful and appealed to a wide range of audiences. She followed up with several more artistic movies that demonstrated a range of acting skills becoming uncommon in Hollywood and even more rare in one so young and attractive. With a tall, athletic physique that still showed all the womanly curves, the auburn hair, and eyes that hovered between green and gray blue, Liz Pendleton was taking the movie industry by a storm.

Liz to her fans and friends, Elizabeth to her mother and grandmother, could not help but reflect on her roots and how much things had changed. Growing up in a small town in Kentucky, she had always been the one to try something different. She could be the tomboy at one moment, the girl that would swim with the boys in the river in cutoff jeans and a tee shirt, or she could be the one playing the princess in the school play and driving the boys crazy. Liz preferred the "realness" of being the boys' friends to the "girly" games that many girls played. She liked to sneak a few beers and dive from the heavy rope that swung out over the river or jump from the rocks of the quarry.

As fun and real as all that was, nothing could compare to standing on the stage and getting a part just right. When she managed that, she could feel the tuning fork of connection thrum in her chest. It was as if she, the character, and the audience were humming in tune to a reality that was unique only to this group and moment in time. After experiencing that one time, she would crave that feeling for the rest of her life. On the occasions when Liz got it perfect, she could see the people in the first few rows beyond the lights shed a tear in one scene or laugh in another. Then they would stand and applaud when it was over. It was a feeling in her chest she couldn't put into words and didn't try. She craved it that way a drug addict craved a fix.

Occasionally, Liz needed some time away to travel and mentally regroup. When she decided she needed to recharge, she just did it and insisted that her staff help support that need. She didn't let people hold her back or run her life. There had been times she tried to push through the fatigue. When she tried that, she found the acting was dead on the inside. That tuning fork didn't thrum, and she couldn't do it the way she needed to. Although she enjoyed the wealth, she was in this for those moments of perfect harmony between her, the audience, and the role. Liz didn't want to kill the ability to make that happen, so she jealously protected her need to recharge.

In the end, she was her own person and a special talent that Hollywood hadn't seen lately. Liz could have the parts she wanted. She could make larger and larger audiences cry and laugh and feel all ranges of emotions before they finally stood and applauded. She could share that tuning fork moment on a national and international scope. That was what she craved.

None of that stopped Liz from being obstinate. When she was younger, people thought she should be more ladylike. She'd been caught on a few occasions drinking and driving trucks with some of the bad boys. Just when they expected she was headed for trouble and her family was ready to intervene, she would surprise them by spending time with her grandmother, listening to the old stories and learning to garden, can, or quilt. She didn't do those things because people wanted or expected it. She did them because she wanted to, and it was what gave her direction and balance.

Now here she was preparing for some other damn event. She was ready to smile for the cameras and say all the right things. Carol, her assistant, and her hair and makeup person Kim were helping her get made up to perfection. They both helped prepare her to talk to the press and the people by reminding her about the event and the latest gossip she might get questioned on. The studio sent over an array of extravagantly expensive dresses from well-known designers for her to choose from.

"Well, this life does have its perks," she mumbled to herself.

She pondered the security people her agent insisted on for this event. With terrorism, demonstrations, and gang violence on the rise, and police shootings happening almost weekly, the world was definitely more chaotic than a few years ago.

Carol poked her head back into Liz's dressing room. "Liz, I'm sorry to rush you, but the driver says we need to leave early to take a different route. He said something about a workplace shooting that we should avoid. It's all over the news."

Liz reached for the remote to the TV near her dressing area and turned it on:

"...heavily armed man and woman dressed for battle opened fire today on a holiday banquet, killing over a dozen and wounding ten. Both attackers were killed in a standoff with police while chanting pro-Islamic state slogans. A local police spokesman says it's too early in the investigation to come to any conclusions about the two shooters and their motives. However, interviews with neighbors of the shooters indicate terrorism as a prime motive. One neighbor tells us she has called the FBI on numerous occasions to complain about the large

number of people and guns going in and out of the couple's residence. FBI officials have yet to comment. We turn to our terrorism expert for her observations related to a possible motive."

The camera switched to a different person.

"Obviously, it's way too early to make any concrete assessment about who these two were and why they did what they did. Nevertheless, I can speak in generalities based on the information at hand and what we do know about these two. Terrorism has spread into America over the last ten to twenty years. With the help of mainstream media sources, most Americans have been able to pretend it doesn't exist. I expect that with these two, we will find some ties to extremism. It's important people understand that most extremists have been indoctrinated since a very young age, and the ideology is reinforced with family, friends, and in the mosques. That level of fanaticism is so foreign to most Americans, they have a hard time fully comprehending it and therefore cannot act or plan appropriately. Add to that the fact that these more fanatical Islamic state organizations have developed a very effective combination of high and low-tech communications for these types of missions. It's likely that although we will find links to fanatical beliefs or organizations, we will not find any direct links to terrorist organizations directing this couple in their plan. The reason I say that is this attack appears to be more of a fervent ideological 'lone wolf' type attack than a concerted effort.

"The Islamic state has chosen to take a different route in these cases. They just publish 'how-to' type plans for terrorist attacks. From there, they leave it up to the teachings of some mosques and organizations to inflame people to the level that they want to carry out an attack. In this day and age, there are always people who are primed to give their life for an attack like this. Then they just choose when and where to carry it out based on their access and motives.

"The scary thing about these types of attacks are they could happen anywhere at any time. They are very hard to stop without giving up some of our civil liberties that we as Americans care so deeply for."

The camera switched back to the reporter.

"Scary thoughts indeed. We will continue to follow this story as it evolves..."

VINCE

Just as he started to let his thoughts wander, the stillness of the morning was interrupted by the frantic barking of the beagle hounds and the sandy blur of a rabbit.

Vince started to raise the Benelli Vinci to take the shot, then changed his mind and lowered it to let the comfort pistol grip hook on his arm while he watched the race. Even though the dogs deserved the reward for their work, this morning was too relaxing and serene to interrupt with a shot. Maybe later.

The Vinci was new, a gift to himself to replace his trusty old Stoegger 2500 12-gauge. While some people didn't like the Stoegger as a cheaper imitation of the Benelli, it had never let him down. With the cost of the Stoegger being so low, he never worried about scratches and falls. The Benelli was in a whole 'nother class. The only two modifications that Vince allowed to the gun were the comfort grip that set the shotgun up to have an AR configuration and a special order external-vented choke from a company down in Georgia that patterned perfectly and further reduced the recoil.

A few yards away stood Vince's friend and hunting buddy Greg, who had been his stepfather's friend before Dan died of cancer. Greg also passed on the shot as the rabbit raced by him about thirty yards further down. Both men were enjoying the cold morning.

Greg and Vince sat down in the crisp grass of a cool winter field in Kentucky, each immersed in their own thoughts. Vince took in the beauty of the Kentucky countryside. He'd spent much of his life in Kentucky, and the beauty of it had yet to be lost on him. It was common for people to begin to take for granted beautiful people and places after a while. Vince still experienced a sense of peace and contentment at the beauty and complexity of nature God had created here.

This farm belonged to a good friend that both men had known for years. They sat on the edge of a grass runway for small airplanes that hadn't been used in years. The owner still kept it mowed, and it was bordered by woods and a small lake. The entire area was teeming with wildlife. Vince could see a Jon boat on the edge of the lake turned upside down and a standalone deer stand at the other end of the field. Most of the crispness of the dawn burned away the frost where the sun struck the grass. While the woods and fields were never truly quiet, it was serene at this time of morning since the animals seemed to rest from the cacophony they created earlier as the sun rose. This put his mind at ease.

The dogs were happy and excited. This was their time of year, and they knew it. It was what they were bred for. Sam, a darker-colored beagle about medium build, was leading the hunt. Right behind him was an active female a little smaller named Ruthie who was colored much like Sam. Greg's dog Tony, who was taller than Sam with more white in his coloring, was right there with them. Occasionally, they did a random bark that said: *"I can smell a rabbit here somewhere."* It was the frantic fast bark that said, *"There he is!"* that Vince and Greg were waiting for.

Vince and Greg stood and spread out with thirty yards or so between them and were kicking at brush and bushes. They needed to help get the rabbits moving again so they could leave a trail for the dogs to follow. It was important to keep in a skirmish type line and keep the guns pointed in a safe direction. They both knew to only take a safe shot, knowing for sure what was beyond the rabbit and that no dogs or people were in range.

Vince was in an introspective mood. For a true outdoorsman, making the kill was only a part of the experience. This was about communing with nature and getting his mind away from work and other stresses. The time outdoors was partially to put his mind in a Zen-like state and partially to practice a skill that made him feel more connected to God and nature. It made him feel more useful and self-reliant as a man, both in body and soul. It was this musing while hunting that prompted Vince to remark to his friend, "Greg, I'm not the man Dan was." He said this without remorse or complaint, merely as a simple observation.

"What do ya mean?" Greg responded, perplexed. "Dan was so proud of you and what you did in the military and for the fine man you've become."

"I appreciate that. Dan was a great man. I learned a lot from him but—"

"But nothing. You're too hard on yourself, and you think too much," Greg said earnestly.

"What I mean is that Dan had all these old world skills that I have no chance to learn now. He knew so much he could have written much of the *Foxfire* books himself."

"You've got more of those skills than you know. And you've got some of your own that Dan didn't have. That's what happens from generation to generation. Some things are lost and others gained."

"Maybe that's true. More than anything Dan was a good man through and through, and I don't think I am." Vince chuckled. "At least I know for a fact I'm not near as good as he was."

"Well, that's a high bar to measure up to. You beat yourself up too much. You're a good man."

"Thanks, that means a lot. I guess what I mean to say is that the older I get and the more I see, I'm convinced that what most people think of as godliness is more about people working together and helping each other and being kind for no reason other than it's right. That's the root of our religion and what Dan lived." Vince spoke more insistently now. "The flip side of that belief is that chaos and activities that drive people apart are evil. Things that make people separate into social groups and stay in their homes or distrust each other are evil in a way that convinces me the devil has a hand in it."

"You're right, there does seem to be a whole lot of that going around," Greg replied thoughtfully.

"Yeah, and that's why I feel the way I do." Vince shook his head. "I want to do good things. I do care about people, but I prefer to be alone a lot or in the woods more. Doing things for people in the community doesn't come as second nature for me as it did for Dan. He was community minded; he had a loving nature that was closer to God. My nature and some of the things I did in the war and after I got home tear things apart more than bind them together. What kind of legacy is that?"

"Life and God have a way of making us the tool we need to be and not the tool we want to be. Relax and enjoy the hunt. You'll do what's right. While you may not be the man Dan was, you're still a better man than you know. Trust in the life and the plan God has for you."

The sporadic barking of the beagles became frantic and was rapidly coming closer. The rabbit was up and running their way fast. Both Greg and Vince stood and spread out, facing the way they knew the rabbit would come. Usually the rabbit would be fifty to a hundred yards ahead of the dogs.

"You shoot him," Greg said. "I don't want to."

"Me either. I'm not in the mood for rabbit meat tonight. Being out here and letting the dogs run is good enough."

"Good." Greg sat back down on the cold ground.

Vince sat beside him and pulled out some beef jerky, offered some to Greg, and they let the dogs run. "I had a call a couple weeks ago from my uncle Dave asking me to join him in a business venture."

"Uh huh," Greg said non-committedly.

"I told him no when he asked me a while back because I thought it was more like a charity thing for family. I was going through the divorce with Ellie too at that time, so I didn't want to take on a project like what he was talking about. I didn't think I'd do a good job."

"I thought you and your uncle Dave got on well?" Greg inquired.

"Oh sure, I think the world of him. We don't see each other often or talk all the time, but that's never bothered us. You know how it is sometimes. He's a heck of a man. Uncle Dave has always been the greatest uncle a kid could have. He worked on airplanes, both in the Coast Guard and in his own business. He would come to our house in Denver and play in the yard with us kids. Sometimes he would take us to dinner when his own brother, my dad, was too drunk or shacking up somewhere and didn't make it home."

"That must have been a hard time for you all."

"I guess it could have been." Vince nodded. "I never thought of it like that. Just...some people had things to deal with. As a kid, I always supposed other people just had different things to deal with is all."

Greg chuckled. "You were probably smarter than you knew, even at a young age."

"Sometimes, for days at a time, we didn't know if we would see our dad or not. We always knew Uncle Dave would be there for us, though. I lost touch with him through the years I was in the Army and after moving back to Kentucky. Even so, he would still stop by out of the blue to have dinner or catch up."

"He sounds like a good man."

"He is. That's what I was getting to. I did help him out on some things he asked me to do."

"What was that?" Greg asked, his curiosity rising.

"He wanted me to try to find a certain type of land to purchase for his company. He had all sorts of requirements, like how close to the city or how far from it. It had to be on high ground, have fields to grow food and support homes. The list was long. When he asked for my help, I knew I couldn't turn him down. The challenge was exciting, and I like looking at farms anyways."

"Me too."

"I should have asked you to come with me," Vince said. "I didn't want to bother you, and I knew you were busy."

"You can call anytime you want, you know that."

"I will next time. Anyway, I worked at it and was lucky to find a large parcel of land that was exactly what Uncle Dave said he was looking to buy."

"Where is it?" Greg asked.

"It's over close to Carrollton where the Little Kentucky River empties into the Ohio. You might remember it from when we hunted there a few weeks back?"

"I sure do! It's a nice place. It was cold hunting that morning with the frosty air rolling up off the river and dusting us with snow. It was good up there for a December morning," Greg said. "I thought the Bradford family had an orchard and farm there, and even a diner?"

"It's always a diner with you." Vince chuckled. "They did. We promised to keep the orchard and farm running and even expand the diner. That's what the family wanted, so it was a perfect fit. You know how it is with a lot of farming families. The younger generation has no interest in continuing the family tradition. The older folks were heartbroken about losing the family farm as a legacy."

Greg nodded. "That's hard."

"Much of the property you can't see has a large family-owned 'pick your own' type farm. They used to produce a lot of what you old timers call 'truck,' or vegetables and fruits that people pay to come and pick."

Greg snickered. "Be careful there, Vince. You're not getting any younger yourself."

"I don't think it would be hard to get that stuff up and running again. They raised some cows and hogs, too. I don't know if you remember, but most of the meals they serve in the family diner contain meat and produce from the farm."

"I know that restaurant. We've eaten there before and liked it. I even ate there a couple weeks back. You say your uncle bought it?"

"You only saw the part of the farm we hunted a couple times. There is a lot more to that property. It has several hundred acres close to the conjunction of the rivers. Uncle Dave's people wanted something about thirty to forty miles out from the city. So it was perfect from a location perspective as well. It was exactly what he was looking for.

"Mmmhmm."

"The Bradfords were still reluctant to sell and see their family farm and business torn down. They didn't want to have all the fruit trees and fields cut down, tilled over, and replaced by buildings and subdivisions. When I told Uncle Dave their concern and reticence to sell, I expected him to ask me to keep trying. I know he doesn't want to hurt people. I expected he would want to make changes to whatever he bought."

"Makes sense. He has to develop the property to make money. He had to get rich somehow."

"That's what I expected, too. However, he was able to secure the deal by promising, and putting it in the contract, that he would only develop a portion of the land. He promised he would keep the farm running much as is. That's along with expanding the diner and keeping it open."

"That's pretty generous."

"Even with all that, the couple that owned the property was still hesitant. They hoped it would be a legacy their children would continue the same way it had been passed on to them." Vince sighed. "I have to give Uncle Dave credit, he didn't pressure them. Yet with one of their kids living in Europe, another in New York, and the last one down in Atlanta, it was unlikely they would come home to run the farm. Each one of them is married and happy in their own careers that have nothing to do with farming. It was unlikely they would return or do anything other than sell their inheritance to a developer later themselves."

"That's sad. Just because that's the way of the family farm nowadays doesn't make it any easier."

"Yes," Vince answered. "It was sad, but Uncle Dave made it a good deal for everyone involved. It met our needs perfectly. We promised to keep it much the same where we could and expand and improve it where it made sense."

"It's a good deal when everyone is satisfied."

"That's true. So once the deal was agreed to verbally, Dave got his lawyers involved, and those guys are sharp. I'm glad they don't work for someone with fewer scruples. Dave had them go through all their paperwork to buy that farm and a few surrounding pieces of property. He even included a payment to me to spend time on the property to familiarize myself with it. He wanted me to help keep people off who shouldn't be there and get to know it like the back of my hand. He said he'll be sending some people out to do some work and I can earn some of the money directing them around."

"Sounds like a good deal. We should ride the property lines on horseback."

"That sounds perfect. They set up a line of credit for the foreman and some of the farm and restaurant workers to keep it all going. Heck, I would have paid *him* for the privilege of having free run of the place."

"Sounds great."

"Uncle Dave didn't want me telling people yet he bought it, so I didn't say much. I was worried that the spot we liked hunting was going to be developed soon. I wanted to enjoy it as much as I could before that happens. I know there are other good hunting spots on that property; I always liked that spot best, though."

"It doesn't sound like they wanted to do much with it."

"That's the thing," Vince said. "Right now, Dave is hell-bent on developing that piece and doing it fast. He's pressing me hard to join his company."

"You mean he is going to break his word and tear it all down?" Greg asked with alarm.

"No, he's going to develop a small part of it. He wants it to fit in and be contained in a limited area. The plan is to keep the orchards, crops, and restaurant intact. He says if I join, I can help assure it all comes out right."

"So are you going to?" Greg asked.

"Honestly, I like my regular job and the pride I get from making it on my own and doing it well. I do love what he has planned there, though, and want to be a part of it. I told him I'd join part time. He agreed but told me that sometime, I'd have a decision to make. I know that day's coming. They've already started with the building project, and they know what they want and how to get it done quickly."

"On another note, Vince," Greg said, ready to change the subject. "You were in the Army. Do you think we could go to war with Russia?"

"Ha, that's a big subject change! Why do you ask that?"

"I was listening to the radio on the way over here. They were going on about Russian fighters in U.S. airspace. U.S. and Russian fighters have faced off over Alaskan airspace several times this month. They said that while Russian incursions into U.S. airspace aren't unusual, the frequency and depth of those incursions lately is concerning. I don't know if the Russians are just testing U.S. defenses or if these incursions are only mistakes. They said this increases tensions between our two countries when viewed through the lens of Russia's history of aggressive moves in the Ukraine and other places."

"Based on my training, I suspect the Russians are doing two things. First, they're testing our reaction time to see how far they can get into our country and how aggressively we respond. Secondly, they are testing our resolve. How much will we take?"

"Why? That's just silly and dangerous."

"The Russians are more pragmatic than us. They know there is a high probability we could go to war someday. It's important to know how much of a head start we plan to give them if they ever do attack. Even cyberwarfare is merely a precursor to boots on the ground for them. They need to know how we will respond. It's smart when you think about it."

"Do you think they would attack?" Greg pressed.

"Probably not." Vince shook his head. "If they did come after us, I don't think they would take the lead. If the Russians ever start to think seriously about attacking us, be wary of them to getting cozier with China or North Korea first. They would want to convince one of them to take the brunt of the first attack. However, you can be sure Russia would find some way to be there when it's all over."

Part Three

CHANGE

"Of the twenty-two civilizations that have appeared in history, nineteen of them collapsed when they reached the moral state that the United States is in now."

- Arnold Joseph Tonybee

LIZ

"Bill, is all this extra security necessary?" Liz asked from the back of the dark SUV.

"Yes ma'am," the bodyguard said. "When the studio and your agent advised you to hire me a year ago, things were different. At most I kept paparazzi away from you and fans from getting too touchy feely. The worst-case scenario we worried about was a stalker. We might have added some security if you were doing a shoot in a location that was less secure. That was about it."

To Liz, Bill was like a brick wall with his emotions and stern, reticent nature. He was a man who, while not so tall, seemed large. Standing close to five nine, his eyes were dark like his hair that was cut short in a military style. He was also thick through the neck and shoulders.

Liz was partially participating in the conversation and letting her mind drift. She rode in the dark SUV with tinted bulletproof windows. She didn't know the driver. Bill was up front in the passenger seat. While some people in her profession thrived on the star treatment, Liz didn't like the way it made her feel isolated from the people and outside world. It was an extravagance to have two vehicles and five men to take one girl to a party.

She knew herself well enough to know that when her mind started to get negative or in this reflective state, she needed to get back to her family and friends in Kentucky to recharge. Hollywood and Southern California had everything a person with access and means could want. However, it was easy to become jaded and emotionally isolated here. Too much separation and star treatment made it harder for Liz to be genuine in her connection with the audience. John, her agent, would be disappointed again and remind her of all the missed opportunities when she told him she wanted to clear a few weeks of her schedule. Yet she couldn't fulfill any commitments if she didn't get her mind right. Liz was adamant that she owed her fans the genuine article and from the heart emotions. She promised herself to never just go through the motions.

"What's so different, Bill?" she asked, shaking her mind from her reverie. "I guess I haven't been paying attention. The news seems pretty much the same as it's always been. I don't hear a huge alarm or concern being raised about terrorism or threats any more than usual."

"Ma'am, it's hard for me to put it into words," Bill spoke in more of a concerned brother tone. "In my opinion, people hate each other more the past few years. They're resorting to violence more and listening less. The two political parties have been able to rile their constituents up to a level that it's like the reds and blues are preparing for war."

"That's politics," Liz chuckled.

"Maybe. I'll be the first to admit I hope I'm wrong. This feels different, though."

"Okay." It was hard for Liz to hide the skeptical tone in her voice.

"It's like this," Bill said. "For thousands of years, it's been hard for people to hurt or kill one another. I know this for certain. We have to train soldiers in the mental approach to killing. Despite all the violence you see on TV, that's a small percentage of the population. Most people are so ingrained in the rules and following the crowd that they would be freaked out by the thought of killing another human being. It's biblical. People either need to be cornered physically or emotionally, or they have to hype themselves up to kill. At least the common man does. Throughout history, that has meant that the tipping point is in the favor of good people who want peace and order.

"Because the bad people were always such a small percentage of society, we could employ a limited police force to keep them in check. If the problem ever got so large that you needed an army-sized police force, then there is something fundamentally wrong with your society. Then you have a police state and the seeds for civil war."

Liz nodded, beginning to understand Bill's point.

"A trained soldier doesn't need the hype to kill after the first or second battle," Bill explained. "There are very few soldiers that can kill dispassionately from the start. You see some of the same casual attitudes toward death and killing in the inner-city gangs. Those gangs and the people in that life are on a constant war footing. With all that in mind, killing is still not normal for most people." Bill was clearly passionate about the subject. "Heck, even whole countries need to build up people to support their views on war with rallies, speeches, and news blitzes. Armies and societies have done that for thousands of years, because it's easier to kill or enslave another group that you hate so much as to think they're practically inhuman. When you demonize the opposition that way, you don't have to listen to them or even acknowledge their alternate point of view."

"Wow," Liz muttered under her breath, beginning to follow what Bill was saying.

"One writer wrote a book called *The Silencing of America,* which sums up a good portion of the disdain we hold for people with different views and how nothing they say can possibly reach our brains. That's part of what's going on in America."

When Bill paused to let Liz reply, she had nothing to say. She fully understood what Bill was trying to get across, and it was scary. Like a marriage when people didn't care enough to even listen to each other anymore.

"You have to totally discredit your enemy and the lines of communication to dehumanize them enough to rile your people up. We're already in a bad place financially as a country. We have other countries and terrorists wanting a crack at us. It's a bad time to have this level of internal strife."

Liz gazed out the window, pondering Bill's words, wondering if he was one of those right-wing nuts, or was he on to something?

Just then she heard pings against the vehicle, and it rapidly accelerated and swerved hard, throwing her shoulder against the door. Liz turned back to see what they had veered so hard for. The second SUV fell back, turning in slow "S" curves in the road, blocking someone from behind who was trying to get past. With an odd sense of detachment, Liz observed the cat and mouse game of the vehicles behind her. The men protecting her were blocking the advance of some bad men with maneuvers that resembled water ballet from inside her vehicle where the sound was muffled. Then G forces pressed her back against the seat as her own vehicle sped up again through an opening in traffic. Bill spoke into his headset urgently, and his whole persona transformed before her eyes. His face, posture, and words were laden with a smoldering intensity. The man she had been speaking to a moment ago as a friend and employee was now so charged she wanted out of his way. She kept her gaze focused on the second SUV as it fell further away. One of the security men rose from its sunroof and another out of a side window to shoot. Both were carrying identical Beretta Storm 9mm assault weapons. While Liz didn't know what they were, she did know they reminded her of something futuristic. She'd seen the weapons earlier and teased Bill that they looked like movie props. Bill chuckled, saying in most situations he preferred a Tavor as an alternative, although the Beretta was a good brand and didn't take up a lot of space. Additionally, the 9mm round didn't carry as far or punch through as much as a .556 or .308

round. In an urban environment, he wanted to minimize risk to bystanders any way he could.

It was the pinging against her vehicle and the trailing vehicle shooting back that made it hit home that she was actually in danger. The fact that they were in the middle of a firefight was unreal and terrifying to Liz at the same time. Her breathing became fast and shallow, and a wave of panic hit her. Her body started to shake as she realized the pings she'd heard earlier were rounds directed at her vehicle. More specifically, they were fired at *her*! A detached part of her noted that this didn't sound like the firefights in her movies. This was real. Liz's most prevalent thought was to get as low as she could. She would have crawled under the seat if she could. The scene both mesmerized and terrified her to the core at the same time. She couldn't tear her eyes away from the fight behind her.

Her SUV couldn't get far away because of the dense traffic. Her mind slowed down and focused on minor details: the spark of light flash from the muzzle of the weapon as the other men fired at the second SUV escorting her; one of her men shooting from the sunroof of the second SUV losing his balance and grabbing for support; a silver minivan trying to get past that second SUV. Men from that minivan were shooting from the windows toward her people. Even further back, she thought she saw a beat-up Honda desperately trying to weave through traffic and catch up. She couldn't tell if they were thrill seekers or part of the ambush team that got left behind in traffic. It was inconceivable that her driver and security folks could be so calm. The thinking part of her brain knew this was their profession. The irrational part thought they were crazy.

It wasn't long before the SUV she was in left the other vehicles behind and things appeared to return to normal and slowed down. Both Bill and the driver acted as if nothing happened. Liz wondered for a moment if Bill's terrible warlike visage had only been in her mind. Still, she knew what she saw. It would stick with her for a long time. It made her glad he was on her side and not against her.

"Bill, what the hell was that? Aren't you worried about the others? Why the fuck are you so calm? Why are you acting like nothing happened?" Liz could hear the hysteria rising in her voice and didn't care.

"Ma'am, this is exactly what we were talking about earlier. Things like this are becoming more common. Carjackings are just one of many things going on. Police aren't responding as fast because so many have quit and the replacements are not trained as well. The older, more experienced officers are leaving, and the new ones are less inclined to put themselves in harm's way. I don't blame them when you consider they're getting sued and shot so frequently for so little pay and support from the people in their own communities. I'm guessing those crooks saw two black SUVs the night of the big gala and assumed someone wealthy would be loaded with jewels and cash and worth trying."

"That's possible," Liz allowed.

"Our men are fine," Bill reported. "They radioed that soon after we got away the minivan broke off and took a side street. There was another beater car further back that followed the minivan when they turned off. Besides, we have bigger questions to deal with." Bill grinned in an attempt to lighten her mood. Some men didn't have the right face smiling.

"What could be bigger than what we just dealt with?" Liz asked, not even trying to hide the high-pitched incredulity in her voice.

"I don't think I've ever heard you say 'fuck,'" Bill said. "It's not like you. You're classier and prettier than that."

"What does being pretty have to do with cussing?" Liz asked, perturbed at being scolded by her security man. "Beside are you saying that's it? They shoot at us and we shoot back and it's over? This is crazy!"

"Yes," Bill said patiently, "that's it. Our people are okay. We don't think we hurt any of them that bad. We've already called the police and informed them why we left the scene. There may be a perfunctory investigation or a lawyer may have to pay a fine for us, but yes, that's it."

"My God, that's insane."

"Yes ma'am, it is. We can go home and skip this event if you like. What's your preference?"

After a pause, Liz said, "Let's see this thing through. And by the way, thank you."

"No problem, ma'am. Keeping you safe is what I do."

"Thank you for what you said about me being classy too."

Arriving at the event, they were ushered through a phalanx of security. The second SUV had caught back up earlier and now peeled off as they approached the red carpet. The SUV gently glided up to the red carpet as if nothing happened. Bill stepped out to open the door for Liz. Her agent John was there to escort from the car, through the throng of paparazzi, and into the event. She supposed she should have allowed some Hollywood hunk to perform that role so the gossip columns could go through their gyrations of who was dating whom. John and the studio execs were always trying to play matchmaker. It was fun sometimes, though usually merely tedious. The men they tried to set her up with were so fake. When she tried to have a heartfelt conversation, it was awkward and strained more often than not.

As a Hollywood star, Liz knew how to put on a winning smile as John escorted her up the red carpet. She was still feeling shaken on the inside. Her heart rate still hadn't slowed, yet none of her fans would have ever guessed. She wanted to get inside somewhere safe and quiet where she could lose her cool for a moment. She needed some time to process why her security team could be so cool with all this and why it wasn't a bigger deal. Had shootouts in the street on your way to work become so commonplace that it didn't warrant much of a reaction anymore? It boggled her mind.

DAVE

With the conclusion of the sanitation workers' strike, the other service disruptions virtually ceased. Dave was glad to be back at the corporate headquarters, although as a business man and citizen, the concessions the politicians offered the strikers amounted to kicking a huge can down the road. The city was accruing debt at a level the economy and tax system couldn't possibly maintain.

At the Cavanaugh Corp headquarters, Dave was both apprehensive and excited about this meeting. They were using the huge mahogany boardroom on the 30th floor. Despite the wealth and size of the Cavanaugh Corporation, the headquarters did not need a huge presence. Most of the people and assets were spread around the country at different work locations, sub offices, and warehouses. Leasing the top ten floors of the new glass office tower in Denver was more a concession to his board than a personal choice for Dave. The offices and location were beautiful and decorated tastefully. While Dave said the soul of his company resided in the Colorado mountains around South Park, he had to admit that the brains of it was here at the top of this office tower.

While technically Cavanaugh Corporation did not own a majority of the building, they did have a significant stake in its ownership and they had built it. Dave had been with the construction crew when they put the final capping I-beam in place. It was an incredible rush to be up there with the construction crew gazing out over the city. He could see the plains off to the east, the majestic Rocky Mountains at his back as he stood on the bones of the incomplete building.

Usually Dave grew annoyed with these types of meetings. He was a man of action. The schmoozing that was such an integral part of his business didn't sit well with Dave and felt phony and cumbersome. However, he was good at it, figuring the reason he did it well was because he didn't like the fake part of it. When he was able to connect with a client on a personal level, then it became more fun. In those cases, they could sit down over a glass of top shelf Kentucky bourbon and dream. Then Dave's true skill kicked in, and that was turning dreams into wood, steel, glass, and concrete realities.

This meeting was different. Leaders, specialists, and lawyers from his company were here, as well as a few hotshot advisors from outside firms they had worked with in the past. These men and women each had specialties in various areas of the plan he wanted to discuss. Their help would be crucial.

"Ladies and gentlemen, let's come to order and get this show on the road." Dave spoke with confidence. "I assume everyone has been briefed on what we want to accomplish here and all the proper non-disclosure agreements have been signed." He glanced over to Andrew Ballard, the head of his legal department. A nod was good enough to allow Dave to keep going. "I know the documents and non-disclosures were a little more restrictive than usual with some added financial and legal penalties. I apologize for that. This endeavor is potentially very big, even by our standards. It's also close to my heart, and I don't want anything to go wrong."

Dave wasn't trying to intimidate; he just wanted to impress on people the gravity of this proposal and what it meant. "If the way we do this and release information is done wrong, it could do incalculable harm to the project. If anyone has any hesitation or misgivings about any of this, please, let's air them today during this meeting."

One of the lawyers Dave didn't know yet cleared his throat, and Dave nodded for him to speak.

"Mr. Cavanaugh, with all due respect, the NDAs were so restrictive and the documents shared with us so vague I'm not quite sure *what* this is you're planning. I can't say for sure if I have any misgivings yet or not."

Dave nodded. "I promise when this day is over, you should know all that you need at a high level. Each of you will be working on separate tasks in smaller groups."

"As long as we aren't doing anything illegal or unethical, I'm on board," the man quipped. "I'm probably on board anyway if the profits are as high as people are speculating." He followed with a snicker, scanning the room to see who appreciated his humor. He found few takers. It was easy to tell this was a guy who thought he was the clever life of the party, and Dave wasn't amused. Still, a few of the attendees nervously laughed with him. The majority averted their eyes as if they were embarrassed for him, even though he didn't have the sense to be embarrassed for himself.

Dave had an impeccable reputation for honesty and ethics. Nevertheless, his face only tightened for a moment before he eased the tension with a smile. "I can assure you I will be leading from in front with my own reputation and money. I promise no one involved with this project has anything to worry about on either account. The purpose and outcome of this meeting could very well launch this venture and give it legs or spell doom for the future of this project I'm calling 'Chartertown.' I expect these towns will be like land-based arks for medicine, religion, knowledge, and stability in the event they're needed that way. Perhaps it's better to call them the Arks or even Arks of America. I will do everything in my power to make this work. I see no reason why it won't be a rousing success."

Dave was an old poker-faced veteran of these types of meetings, yet this time it was hard not to let his emotions show. In short, he was asking the group to devise a totally new way for people to own a home, participate in a company, and invest in mergers and acquisitions, rolled up into one packaged endeavor.

That's not exactly true either, he thought. This was a way for them to buy into a whole new way of life.

"Let me take a few moments and give you the highlights of my plan, then I'll turn it over to my more capable staff to get further into the details. What I'm proposing is a four-pronged approach from a business perspective. Most of what I'm going to say to you will have some elements of it that should be familiar. When they are combined in a plan such as this is when it really changes things."

Dave paused for a moment and let his eyes travel the room, taking inventory of the interest of the crowd. They appeared to be hanging on to his words closely. "I believe that the purpose and approach is unique and noble. Think of today like an opportunity to start a brand-new company from the ground up with four divisions, or verticals. In essence, that's exactly what we're doing. What will be new is how we combine what we're doing and how we use it. I like to think of this much the same way people would have when a fleet of ships was dispatched to build a colony in the new world more than two hundred years ago. It is often overlooked in history that those ships and goods were sometimes paid for by people who were investing in hopes of a huge reward. The history books only remember the bold and noble people coming to the new world to escape the oppression of the old in hopes of something better."

Dave saw some smiles and nods. "I feel superbly confident that this venture will be successful financially, but that's not the huge reward I dream of. The legacy I hope to attain with this endeavor will be to create a series of towns, of sorts. They will be modern day refuges in case the world does go to hell. They will be arks to protect seeds, medicine, art, and religion. More importantly, they will be there to protect the very people who will help us start over again if or when things finally go downhill. If we are successful in the way that I imagine, people won't need to start over from scratch. We will be able to jumpstart this nation from a solid beginning." Dave's voice rose steadily, his passion such that he couldn't hold back. Some in the room were caught up in the moment and did a subdued cheer. Others appeared uncomfortable, as if they were somehow caught up in a prayer group they hadn't planned to attend. Dave wanted the people who were enthusiastic to catch on and share his vision.

"Things were hard for the early colonists in America, the same as they were hard for Noah and his family after the flood. Noah had an ark supplied with everything he needed, along with the aid and counsel of God. Can you imagine how much harder it would have been for the early American colonists without supplies and equipment from Europe? Think about making a plow without an operating mine or factory to smelt the ore. Try contemplating what the world would have been like for Noah without the supplies and shelter provided because of the guidance from God. Think about the bounty Noah preserved through the flood."

Dave looked around the room before continuing. "I know many of you view the stories of the Bible with skepticism. That's fine; I'm not here to preach to you. Still you need to keep this in mind: millions of people do believe in those stories. What's more, you need to know this with certainty," he paused to make eye contact and emphasize this fact, "no nation stands forever. It has never happened in the history of the world. That's a fact, hard and true. You can believe in this plan for the profit or believe in it as an ark to preserve people and wisdom in the floods of chaos that will come. You can even choose to believe in this plan as a lifestyle. It is a way to preserve some of a more idyllic or moral way of life that is passing us by. I hope you believe it for all of those reasons to some degree or another. No matter how you get here, I promise you, it will work!"

The room got quiet. There was no cheering this time and no postures of dissent either. They were all a bit stunned.

"Okay, enough of my ramblings. Let's get to work."

Dave sensed they were relaxed and decided to turn the meeting back to a more businesslike approach.

"The first prong of this plan is more of a real estate transaction. Most of the property held in this part of the plan will be in a hybrid gated community concept. We will talk more about that in a moment.

"The second prong is more like a major mutual fund I want to set up. It will have a fund manager, team, and follow all the regular processes for a major mutual fund. The only difference is that this fund will focus specifically on goods and services that your prepper type would find useful. Aside from my own views, this is a hot industry right now, and we will get into this more later as well.

"The third prong is probably more closely related to the second. In this venture, we will take a controlling interest of some of the companies we would normally invest in as a part of the mutual fund. We know from experience that many companies are not managed well. We can increase our profits by improving the leadership teams where appropriate. I would be happy to have the factories and distribution centers for those types of goods close to our communities. In as many places as makes sense, we would move appropriate businesses, like medical offices or a wood stove distribution facility close to our arks. Combining that with what we are doing in prong one is just practical. We will try to make the businesses symbiotic with the communities and have a cache of goods close at hand."

Dave glanced around and found most people were frantically taking notes.

"The fourth and final prong is the path to ownership in these communities. As we build these gated communities, I'm proposing that we don't resell the properties as we normally would a home or office building. Instead, I propose that we sell ownership shares and access to the facilities much like a country club sells member access in an equity agreement. Obviously, this is a much more complex and different than people are used to when it comes to home ownership. I know people would want different levels of ownership or membership. Some people will want larger homes, and others would be content with an apartment. Let's not forget this is still America, and capitalism works when it's not overburdened with too many rules and regulations."

That comment garnered some of the smiles Dave was hoping for. "As a part of this plan, I want to give certain people substantial discounts to join the charter towns who have skills we want in the community. That's where you all come in. I need a plan for how we price this and what type of fee structure we should put in place. I need to know what's appropriate and will work for the initial deposits or initiation fees. I know some states will be easier to work in than others due to local laws and regulations. I'll need your advice along those lines as well."

"Mr. Cavanaugh, do you intend to underwrite this totally on your own?" questioned one of the men Dave recognized, though couldn't recall his name. "What is the financial scale you see for this venture?"

"I intend to be the figurehead and the largest investor," Dave answered. "I have no intention of funding this entirely on my own. That is not to say that I don't believe in this with all that I am. I just feel that if investors and common people alike don't see the value in what I'm proposing, then I don't want to prop it up artificially myself."

Another woman in the back stood up. "How big do you see this getting, Mr. Cavanaugh?"

"If we have the time and things go as I think they might, I could see several charter towns in each state down the road. Long term, I could see perhaps a couple hundred nationally. It's possible the mutual fund could turn over billions financially. To that end, I see no reason why we couldn't soon be managing a division of extremely profitable companies. Most of those companies would be low tech with a very manageable cost structure. That's not to say we wouldn't have a few high-tech companies mixed in as well. Those would be related to mobile medicine, solar, or wind power concepts. Who knows what else?"

The lady who spoke up previously pressed on. "Mr. Cavanaugh, I have heard you mention these communities both as charter towns and as arks. Can you enlighten us a little bit more on the difference as you see it?"

Dave chuckled. "You're right, I guess that is confusing. I haven't settled on what to call them yet. I have toyed with the term Chartertown, and in truth that's probably closest, because in each community it will be the people who determine their bylaws and direction, within a scope we allow, of course. These towns will be safe, walled refuges for people to ride out the storm of chaos I suspect is coming. Arks hidden in plain sight."

The same lawyer who asked about ethics earlier spoke up again, his tone sarcastic. "Mr. Cavanaugh, forgive me, but this all sounds like some type of doomsday bugout plan. The only difference being that it's on a much grander scale than most people would dream of or have access to. How do you propose we respond to that type of feedback when more of this becomes public?"

"I can see how a few shortsighted people could make that mistake. I do think this country is in decline and want us to have a plan. However, make no mistake," Dave said seriously, "I am a businessman. I will not deceive or defraud my investors and business partners." After a few seconds' pause and locking eyes with the impertinent lawyer, the young man finally dropped his eyes to his notepad. "This company and these investments will make money. They will be profitable. These communities will be clean and virtually crime free. For some people, they will harken back to a simpler time. There is nothing about this proposal I am ashamed of."

A few people in the room mumbled approval. Most of the others nodded in agreement.

"And yes, to answer your question, I do believe in being prepared. I enjoy some of the more rustic skills like camping, hiking, and occasionally shooting. And yes, I do enjoy some hunting and the study of traditional food preparation or canning and pickling techniques. However, to label me a doomsday prepper is a bit inflammatory. That invokes the image of a slightly paranoid man living in a cabin in the woods with tons of food and ammunition. If that were true, I do have the means to prepare and entertain that type of lifestyle on a grand scale if I so choose. I don't need these communities for myself. I am happy alone in the mountains.

"However, consider this: if you think back through history, men with a little bit of vision and historical knowledge have very frequently known when to vacate a city before a war, plague, or economic decline. Those men have known when to sell out of a company or leave a neighborhood or business before it goes down. I see myself as one of those men and this situation no different. Think of England before the Romans left or Pompeii before the volcano.

"What I do know is that countries don't die on the timeline that companies do. People, companies, neighborhoods, and countries live and die on different schedules. The life of a fly is a day or so. A sea turtle can live fifty to a hundred years. It can take centuries for a country to die, or it can happen in the blink of an eye. I like to think that *if* something bad did happen in this country, I wouldn't have to retreat to a cabin in the woods with two years of MREs. I would hope to live in a community of like-minded people. I would hope to find an oasis of calm in a sea of chaos. I pray that we could have a place that has schools, art, culture, laws, and literature. I would want doctors and medicine on hand if one of you got sick. Most of all, I would want a place of worship and people of faith and community to share with."

Dave paused to take a drink of water. "In times of change and upheaval, people reveal their true nature. Many people promote chaos. While I believe that chaos is evil, I don't think many of the people doing chaotic or destructive things during those times of turbulence are inherently evil, even though the results can be just as bad.

"Where I and some of the prepper types differ is that I don't think all people will be destructive during times of turmoil. I do believe in the goodness of man. Good people will band together and help each other. Many of them will try to feed and protect each other. Those people will try to preserve religion, art, education, and medicine. I believe they will need a safe haven to do so. They will need people of strength to organize and protect them. If things do go south, I hope to have communities spread throughout the country, each as an ark in a sea of chaos.

"All too often the doomsday preppers, as you call them, get too caught up in the entertaining melodrama of a man and his guns and food, in the woods protecting himself, his wife, and his kids. It's easy to enjoy the story and admire that man's heroism. Yet, is it truly heroic to merely survive? Shouldn't we also try to thrive? To only feed yourself, and not plan for our kids, grandkids, and neighbors doesn't feel heroic to me. I think they deserve to live in and enjoy a world similar to what we have. There are good things about this world and our current lives we shouldn't forget. It's the legacy we owe the next generation."

Dave knew he'd already made his point. He was too far off track from the presentation and too involved in what he wanted to say to stop now. Sometimes being the boss did have its privileges.

"It's too easy to forget that we as a people are at our best when we help each other and band together as a group. How long can that one man or one family alone in a cabin in the woods last? What type of world will his kids, friends, and neighbors live and grow up in with no schools, churches, or hospitals? Isn't it more heroic to create something that endures and nurtures the best of what we are as a race?

"Never forget that it can take a country many years to decline. If you're not paying attention to the signs, it can be happening all around you and you won't be ready to respond appropriately when it suddenly changes from a gradual decline to a sudden, more serious situation. These types of declines can be insidious and gradual. When something disastrous does happen, all the people don't die off and disappear like the cliff dwelling Indians or the people of Atlantis. The people that survive go into a transitional period of turmoil and strife. It's like the people of England when the Romans withdrew that I mentioned a moment ago. It could even be a bit like the people of Greece or Egypt today.

"I don't expect these communities to be needed as an ark for many years. I hope they're never needed that way. In the meantime, we will create some great communities to live in. While doing so, we will create a very profitable business that invests in and produces some very decent and high-quality products. These communities will allow people the enjoyment of camping, shooting, hiking, or whatever they want to do. At the same time, people can participate in green living activities as we build energy-efficient homes. People will enjoy our communities as a new and refreshing way to live. They will make money investing in our mutual fund, and they will enjoy purchasing some very sound products.

"If no one else has any questions..." Dave didn't pause or make eye contact. It was clear he didn't want to take any more questions. "...the fine people from my staff can break you out into your working groups to get started on making this happen."

As one group headed off to a different conference room, Dave asked Louis and a few others to stay behind for a moment. While he waited for the others to move out of the room, he stood at the huge window surrounded by mahogany-paneled walls. His back to the room, he gazed off in the distance at the gold-covered rotunda of the Denver capitol building. His eyes focused wistfully at the Rocky Mountains in the distance beyond the capitol.

As was Dave's nature, he could never contemplate at a city, a home, or farm and not envision what it once was and how it evolved. In Denver, he liked to think of an early settlement at the base of the mountains with dirty streets and wooden buildings. He could envision a time when only a few buildings were erected with brick or stone. He could see the Colorado River nearby. A town filled with rugged people who dared to come west. Some of them were good people who banded together to protect and build; others were bad people who were just as rugged but preyed on others and stole or killed.

Dave knew that with time, the good people usually won out. It was what happened during that time of struggle before the good people won out that worried him. He wanted to protect against and mitigate how long the time lasted before the good people won out. He thought that how hard those times got and how long they lasted determined how much was lost in terms of goodness. They needed to preserve all they could. In reality, the longer good people fought the bad, the more of themselves, their progress, and inherent goodness they lost.

The room was quiet, and Dave turned to the remaining group. "You are the best in your professions at what you do. The task I'm asking this group to take on is the most delicate. Each of the other groups has a lot of work in front of them. Their work is made up of tasks that have been done before. In taking on the fourth prong-related ownership positions of these communities, I'm asking you all to figure out how to do the one part of this that has not been done before to my knowledge. I am asking you all to take the biggest leeway or the most creative approach and help me solve this last problem. I know it can be done. You are the people that I know will make it happen."

"Mr. Cavanaugh," one person said, "I've read the brief, and I think I understand what you're shooting for. I'm not sure this can be done all over the country and in every state or municipality."

"That's okay," Dave said. "Figure out where and how it can be done for now. That's the start we need. My preference is to start both here in Colorado and in Kentucky for now. After that, I'd like to bring on a few other locations. Then we can address each situation on a case-by-case basis."

"Okay, Colorado I get," the same person said. "It's your home and has plenty of places that meet your criteria. Your connections are so strong here. I don't think they would deny you anything. But why Kentucky?"

"Good question." Dave smiled. "I'll admit there is a bit of whim in the choice. Mostly it's just that I want it. I'll give you a few other reasons as well. First, I have some people lined up that area that I have complete faith in. I trust them implicitly, and I'm sure they will make it a success. Second, the state is not overly crowded and has an abundance of natural resources. The cost of labor for companies we bring on is not high, and it fits the profile perfectly. Third, local people would welcome this kind of endeavor warmly. That will make the proof of concept I'm asking you to develop easier. What I'm building in Colorado doesn't exactly fit the long-term model. Finally, each community has to be able to stand on its own merits. Kentucky is too far for a convoy of trucks to reach from Colorado in a critical resupply mission. Yet in a worst-case scenario, we could get an airplane there. That means the Kentucky location would be forced to mostly stand on its own in a location well suited for that."

"Why is it important that the communities stand on their own? If that's so important, couldn't we just build a handful of these communities in or near the cities bordering the Rocky Mountain range?" another person in the group asked.

"It's important to me that we make this available across the country. If things ever did go bad, we wouldn't want large waves of refugees beating down the doors of the nearest ark location or charter town. The people who come *after* a disaster are not the planners and builders. They are not the people who typically are able to overcome adversity, survive, and thrive. By and large, those types of people would become a tribe of locusts. By expecting these communities to stand on their own and forcing autonomy of community on them, they can't waste their resources and then hope to go knock on the door of the next community down the line asking for handouts like the other people who didn't plan well."

"I understand," the person said. "I'm totally on board. We should be able to find a plan to make those two states work. After that, I'm sure we can find a few more good locations without delay. I assume you want the ownership process and rules to be similar from state to state, or as much as the various state and local laws will allow?"

"Yes," Dave answered, "with one exception. The concept of a charter town is such that the members will be able to have a great deal of self-governance. They should be very involved in writing and ratifying their own community mission statement. Still, as owners with a controlling interest, we will always have final say and majority ownership in every community. That doesn't mean we won't allow each community to shape itself in as much of its own way as possible. It means we will not give up control so that this grand plan can be deviated from."

"That could be dangerous, sir," another person said, obviously concerned. "What's to stop some hate organization from building the membership core somewhere and discriminating? They could create their own mini kingdom or worse while managing our charter town."

Dave's eyes got hard. "Me. I will stop them. My vision will not be perverted." Then his countenance softened. "And you good people, too. Remember, this only works when good people band together. I would be okay with a community that was mostly Jewish or predominately black or Hispanic. I would be fine with a community of gay and lesbian folks, or people who ride horses or dune buggies or whatever. I would prefer them all mixed together, of course. In any event, each of those communities must abide by our rules. We have the right and obligation to provide rules and oversight to make sure prejudice does not happen. All people will be accepted equally. Each community will practice the core tenets of what this is all about. I'm counting on you all to help me build those rules and safeguards.

"First, I need you all to find a way for us to own shares in real estate and set up a tiered system for people to pay dues or fees for the shares similar to an equity country club's dues. Still, this will be so much more than that because they will be buying an equity position in a home and full lifestyle. They will have a home and way of life that is more insulated from the real world. Like Mayberry behind walls in modern times. If we do this right, it will have so much more benefit than old-fashioned home ownership. As a part of their dues and fees, they would also be getting shares in the mutual fund and business ventures.

"Members would have both financial and service commitments back to the community as a part of their monthly or annual obligations. They would have a say in the government and charter of their own community. To a lesser degree, their ownership position would grant them participation in decisions as shareholders for the company as a whole. It's a very ambitious undertaking legally and something that not only has never been tried, but to my knowledge never even been dreamed of."

"We can make this happen, sir," said the woman who had asked the most questions. "We only need a little time to work out the details. I share your vision."

Beaming, Dave thanked them. "Okay, perhaps this has been dreamed of. However, if it was, it had to be by some hippies in the seventies while building a tent city for a whole other purpose."

After leaving the meeting, Dave sat in his car listening to the news coming from the radio up front:

"...narrowly avoided a downgrade in the U.S. national debt rating this week. Internal experts reaffirmed America's AA+ rating. In 2011, the rating was reduced from AAA, outstanding, to AA+, excellent. While to most Americans the national credit rating doesn't seem impactful to their everyday life, nothing could be further from the truth. Nearly everything we buy is at some level serviced by debt tied to our national rating. If this rating is lowered, the cost of our loans goes up and the cost of goods would skyrocket and create a depression.

"We have only to examine the recent example of Greece to see the impact of a reduction in available money and goods and what increase in the cost of money did to their economy. We could see gas prices that approach ten dollars a gallon and similar increases with food staples such as milk or bread. Unemployment could triple, causing further ripple effects of hyperinflation. This would deplete social resources on an already overtaxed U.S. government and in turn cause more taxes or civil unrest. While some experts say this is a very unlikely scenario, others warn that it's much more likely than people care to admit..."

VINCE

After a long day at the office, Vince packed up his laptop and headed home to the suburbs.

Like millions of other Americans, Vince worked in a cubicle farm, the type of place ridiculed in the *Dilbert* cartoons. Vince had worked his way into a middle management role that afforded him an office with a window view of the Ohio River fifteen floors below. He was good at the job, just not so good at the schmoozing that was so critical to success in corporate America. The popular corporate term was "networking." Vince reflected on his office at the knickknacks and awards. They made him feel connected to the people around him and the years invested in this work. He was most fond of the things people brought him from their travels. Those were special because coworkers and employees didn't have to give him anything; they did it because they were good people and they cared. He had souvenirs from various states and South America, as well as Russia and many from India. For as much as Vince appeared to be outgoing, he kept a large part of himself private, and that could make people think he was standoffish at times. These reminders that people did care made him smile.

Vince pulled into the large driveway of what had been their dream home. It was large and built for entertaining with the requisite man cave, pool, and a wraparound porch on the main level. There was another wraparound porch outside of the turret at the top level. Built to accommodate seven or eight cars, these days the driveway was empty except for his truck.

The house wasn't as clean as it should be. It felt empty and hollow, not worth the effort. Vince walked through the house, noticing the fast food cartons piling up in the garbage, dust and mail on the counter, and laundry to do. He loaded some clothes into a basket, still unsure how Ellie kept the colors from bleeding together and how she made the clothes smell good. It was sheer luck so far that no one at work or the gym had commented that his t-shirts were no longer white, but a lovely shade of pink. Vince now understood at a visceral level the difference between a *house* and a *home*. He needed to fix it up and sell it, perhaps buy a small hobby farm further out of town. He'd been working long hours at the office and could always find a good reason to put it off a little longer.

He hadn't yet gotten over the divorce from Ellie, or Eleanor as she now preferred to be called. He'd lost so much already. Selling the house was just one more link to the past and his marriage he wasn't quite ready to sever.

Ellie was still an attractive woman as she moved into midlife. She had curves she wanted to reduce yet men still noticed with appreciation. She wore her hair shorter these days, and the color ranged from dark blonde to light brown, colored for the season. She had blue eyes that made her and Vince resemble brother and sister more than husband and wife.

The divorce was now two years in the past. Although they'd both known it was coming for quite some time, they kept working at the marriage. Ellie had worked at it because she was a caring person and desperately wanted to make it work. Vince went through the motions of working on it because his head was elsewhere and he foolishly thought things would work out for him the same as they always had. This time there wasn't a stroke of good luck or magical reprieve. In the end, the damage was already done.

After the divorce, Ellie began dating a man named Malcolm she'd met through work. They got along, he was a good man, and he made her happy. Although Ellie first met Malcolm while still married to Vince, he never believed she'd been unfaithful. That wasn't Ellie's way. In an odd way, Vince was pleased that Ellie and Kate were with Malcolm. Chicago could be a dangerous city at times; he would worry even more if they didn't have someone to look out for them. No matter what happened between him and Ellie, he wanted them safe and happy.

According to Kate, Malcolm had grown up in a hardworking north shore family in Chicago. His father owned a mechanical shop that did various engine repair and light machine shop work. Although Malcolm grew up helping his father in the shop, it was his father's dream that his son get an education and a white-collar job. Malcolm was a large man, and strong. He had been born with strength and built it even more working in his father's shop. Because he was large, it was easy for some people to miss that he had kind eyes and a good heart. His resting face could appear meaner than he intended, and it touched Malcolm deeply when Ellie saw past that to who he was underneath.

It was that heart that helped direct his career choice into human resources when his father insisted he not follow him in the family business. Malcolm liked helping people and giving them a sense of purpose. Now Malcolm was a director in the HR department of the company where Ellie worked. When Vince heard that, he teased Ellie about the office romance. Ellie hadn't appreciated the humor, insisting in her tightlipped way when she was upset that everything was on the up and up and they disclosed their relationship early on. Still, it was hard for Vince to think of his wife and daughter spending dinnertime with another man.

When Ellie and Malcolm married, she and Kate moved to Chicago. Kate was excited because she loved the big city. She'd wanted to go to school at the University of Chicago for years. When Vince and Ellie were together, he'd always thought he would have more time to convince her to choose a college closer to home, dreading her going to school in the big city. His fears were partially for her safety, though he also worried she would get a job in another city and be distant from him forever.

He still missed Ellie and their life together. Even more so, he missed Elizabeth Kate. She would always be Kate to him. Vince could remember all the times they had done father-daughter things together as if it were yesterday. It was odd how some memories dimmed, while others stayed vibrant for many years. It seemed only yesterday she was young enough to ride in Daddy's truck and be his best buddy. She loved their special trips to an amusement and waterpark about an hour west of Louisville.

It was hard to contemplate Kate as an adult, nineteen years old, going on twenty-five and living in Chicago with her mother. Thinking of a mature Kate enrolled at the University of Chicago was drastically different from the little girl in his mind. Kate had always wanted to be a lawyer. She was doing great academically and well on her way, now enrolled in political science classes with plans of going to law school in a few years.

When Vince and Ellie spoke on the phone, he wanted to ask what they knew of the big story that was all over the news about a Chicago police shooting. Although those were no longer uncommon, this was a bigger story and getting more coverage. Ellie insisted that he was overreacting and looking for things to be paranoid about concerning Chicago, bringing up the latest trouble in Louisville as an example that there was trouble all over. No city was immune from strikes, riots, and police shootings these days. Vince couldn't disagree. He would have loved for Kate and Ellie to live a more rural, safe life. At the same time, it wasn't fair to take a whole generation and put them "on the bench" from the life their parents and grandparents had enjoyed in an effort to keep them safer.

With the TV droning on in the background, he tried to clean up the house some. He had already heard the current "breaking" news story several times. Every local news station was replaying it and putting their own spin on it:

"We have breaking news. The peaceful march protesting the shooting of Edwin Watson, who was pulled over for simple drunk driving, turned violent today as marchers left the approved route and spread into side streets and nearby businesses.

"Two officers were cut off by the crowd and pelted with rocks and bottles. As tensions escalated, the officers opened fire on the protesters, killing one man. That victim's name has yet to be released. The officer involved has been identified as twelve-year veteran policewoman, Officer Tanya Johansson. A Louisville Metro police spokesperson issued a statement saying the officers involved saw a gun and were trying to protect their lives, as well as those citizens in the immediate area. No gun was found after the crowd cleared.

"In separate news, the police spokesperson issued a statement saying that for the immediate future they will stop responding to certain non-emergency calls in parts of the city, citing manpower issues and the inability to guarantee the safety of their officers. Police urge citizens in the impacted areas to file a report online. An officer will be dispatched within forty-eight hours.

"Civil rights leaders have yet to respond to this latest announcement. The expectation is that riots and civil unrest will not subside anytime soon.

"The governor released a statement that says all options, including the deployment of the National Guard, are being examined. Some experts have warned that the National Guard is underfunded and understaffed at this time. They have openly suggested that if the governor did make the call, many guardsmen would not report. It is suggested that for this reason, along with the long-standing rift between the mayor and the governor, the state may choose to delay a decision on this crisis. Spokespeople for both the mayor and the governor adamantly deny that assertion..."

The leadership for Vince's division at the company in Louisville called a Friday afternoon department-wide meeting to address employees' concerns related to safety.

Vince was not surprised the atmosphere in the room had a frantic tone. What was most alarming was that these white-collar workers, many of whom had known each other for years, were taking sides, visibly separating in the large conference room. Many automatically assumed the police shooting was racially motivated. What was worse was the unspoken assumption that their white coworkers were a part of the problem or against them and siding with racist forces. While Vince knew racism existed, at the same time he was hard pressed to find the racial motivation here. There was a particular element of the crowd made up of Indian workers that was more nervous and confused. It was clear that many Indian workers didn't comprehend the passions and reason for the deep-seated racial divide and why their coworkers had changed so drastically almost overnight. Watching them, Vince thought if things got worse, they would be a community lost and alone.

In an effort to appease people and try and make them feel safer, leadership decided to allow the entire department to work from home the following week and would be sending out communications from the various emotional support groups that people could reach out to with questions and for help. The company had dozens of special interest support groups. Vince would be the only demographic without a support group had he not been in the military. No company in the country would risk the public outcry of creating a special interest or support group for his demographic.

Shuffling out of the large conference room, Vince was approached by Luke Whitner, who used to work in his area. "Vince, are you going to have all your people work from home?" Luke asked.

"I'll give them that option. I don't want anyone to feel like they have to come in if they don't feel safe. I'd feel horrible if someone tried to come in and got hurt."

"Are you coming in then?"

"Some of the time at least. If anyone else is coming in, I feel like I should. It may not matter anyway. If this goes on longer or gets worse, the company will probably make working from home mandatory. They don't want lawsuits on their hands if people get hurt coming in to work."

"Our entire department is working from home now. I'll run by your house a time or two if you want," Luke offered.

"Thanks. We're both far enough out from downtown that we should be okay, but I'd appreciate it," Vince said.

On the way home, Vince decided to stop by both a Kroger and Costco in the vain hope they were open and the shelves were not picked clean. He kept a large supply of survival food from Wise, Mountain House, and Augason Farms, as well as some military surplus MREs. It would be good to buy more if he could. He also decided he would stop by the local Bass Pro and Cabela stores. Mostly he just liked walking through those stores. He already owned most of what he wanted or needed. Camping, survival gear, and ammo would be worth its weight in gold if the current crisis didn't end soon.

Part Four

TAKING SHAPE

"The ability to direct individual accomplishments toward organizational objectives. It is the fuel that allows common people to attain uncommon results."

- Andrew Carnegie

"Riots in the city have grown worse. Louisville police have now been working overtime for six days and are becoming fatigued. The mayor and police chief have warned they are expanding the areas that will be partially served for only the most violent or urgent crimes. For a list of those areas and which emergency calls will get an immediate response, police are asking citizens to go online and read the documentation to complete an incident report. For a link to that site and information, please visit our website.

"In related news, citizens' complaints are rolling in that home invasions, physical assaults, and looting are running unchecked. The police chief insists they are responding to those calls and doing the best they can. Reports to this station by victims relate response times of two to three hours. Some calls have taken as much as two days to get a response..."

Prospect, KY

"Jim, someone is at the door," Laura said with some concern in her voice. It wasn't odd to have a delivery or service person knock, but they hadn't been getting deliveries or service calls lately.

"I'll get it. It's probably someone who is lost or broke down." Answering the door, Jim noticed two men dressed more like they belonged in the inner city than the suburbs. "Can I help you?"

"Yes, we are low on gas and saw your car out front. Can you give us some?" said the smaller of the two with yellow teeth and wispy facial hair, too patchy to be called a beard.

"No, I'm sorry. I only have about a quarter of a tank, and most of the gas stations are closed," Bill said, starting to close the door.

The larger of the two put his arm against the door, stopping Bill from shutting it. "How about we look in your garage for a tank of gas we might use?" the smaller man countered with an unnerving smile as he craned his neck to see past Bill to his wife Laura and their daughter Sarah.

"No," Bill said, trying to sound firm or commanding, yet his attempt at strength was betrayed by a quaver in his voice. "You should leave now or I'll call the police."

"No, you won't call the police, and even if you did, I doubt they'll come," the smaller man said as they strode into the house past Bill's feeble protests. "Your wife can make us something to eat and then we'll poke around for gas or whatever else we need. If you all are nice to us, then we'll be on our way in a little while."

The terror on Laura and Sarah's face escalated to pure panic as the men barged in and eyed them lewdly. Bill didn't own a gun and couldn't fight these men. He was afraid for his wife and daughter. His son Jimmy was downstairs playing video games with headphones on. "Sure...O-Okay," Bill stammered, hoping to appease them and give them some food so they would go away. "Laura can make something for you. Sarah, go to your room so these men can eat."

"No, Sarah can stay here. I like having her where I can see her." The smaller man grabbed Sarah by the forearm. "Come sit in my lap, honey."

"She's only fifteen!" Bill yelled, lunging forward. The larger man hit him across the jaw, crumpling him to the floor, and proceeded to kick him savagely in the face and ribs until he was unconscious, laughing as Laura and Sarah screamed.

The commotion roused Jimmy from the basement, and he came running upstairs to see his sister in the creepy man's lap, a gun pointed at his face. "Now stand still! Is anyone else in the house?" the small man said, his voice rising in pitch, clearly getting angry and mean, the pretend genial demeanor totally gone. "Bruce, tie up the man in case he wakes, and the boy in the other room there too. I think Laura and Sarah here will be real sociable for a while."

Later, Bill woke to the screams and cries of his wife and daughter. He was able to free himself and tried to creep into Sarah's room behind the man called Bruce with a large kitchen knife. His mind didn't comprehend the meaning of his wife's change in screams from the other room until a split second before the bullet entered his brain through the back of his skull.

"Bruce, finish what you're doing there with the young one, then tie her up. I'll knock the mom out and we'll grab whatever food and gas we can find and leave. I doubt anyone will come to a single shot. We're pretty much done here anyway."

LIZ

During a break in the media event, Liz leaned in and whispered, "Carol, are we close to being done yet?"

Liz was impeccably dressed, all the while making the outfit appear casually thrown together. She wore fashionable jeans, a blouse with a plunging neckline, and high-heeled brown ankle-high boots. Her jewelry accented the outfit perfectly, her hair carefully mussed.

Liz made it through all the tedious interviews and media events her agent John arranged and, Carol told her, "*simply couldn't be missed.*" She did it with such style and grace that many didn't know how much she disliked this part of her career. She was aware she'd been too flippant and a bit caustic toward reporters lately. Liz recently asked her team to arrange a break in her schedule, and as much as she needed it, she couldn't make it happen for a few more weeks. She had a short cameo role to perform in Hollywood at the studio and some public service announcements to film. On top of all that, she was scheduled to attend a mysterious soiree planned for the following weekend that occupied her mind.

"You're almost done," Carol soothed. "You're doing great, and they love you. The studio will be happy. Each one of these events improves your Q-score numbers."

"Yes, but at what cost?" Liz muttered under her breath. She got through the rest of the event with a wide smile and an engaging sense of humor.

During the ride home, Liz stared out the window of her SUV, letting her mind drift, absentmindedly, pondering for perhaps the tenth time the mysterious soiree.

"Carol, I need you to make sure we get that time scheduled off that we spoke of for a few weeks in Kentucky later this month or early next. Cancel whatever you need to in order to make it happen." Her voice came out more as a command than she'd intended, which only strengthened her resolve to get away.

"That will put a hole in the promotions for your upcoming film. The studio and your publicist will be disappointed."

"They will just have to be disappointed then." Liz made a conscious effort to soften her tone. "Tell them I'm being a diva. If they want me happy and smiling at the events, then they need to help make it happen."

Carol nodded and started typing into her smartphone, her thumbs and fingers a blur.

Liz leaned forward and tapped Bill's shoulder. "Bill, you don't need to come along for this trip if you need some time off. I'm sure someone else can go. I'll be covered by studio security most of the time and flying into the smaller airport, Bowman Field in Louisville. My family will be there to meet me."

"I'd rather keep you safe than take the time off," Bill answered after a moment of thought. "On the other hand, my son is out of school on break soon, and my ex-wife has been talking about summer camp. I think he's still too young for summer camp, but not too young for a camping trip with his dad. So if you're sure it will be okay, I'll take you up on your offer and be here when you get back."

Liz grinned at the boyish smile that crept onto Bill's face when he spoke about his son. "This will work perfectly then. Bring back pictures. I grew up camping with my family and love it."

She leaned back and touched Carol's knee, forcing her to look up from her smartphone. "So tell me what you know about this soirée weekend after next."

"I have no idea," Carol said. "It sounds so exciting, mostly because they're keeping it so secretive. When John urged you to attend, I was glad I didn't have to go too. I thought it would be so boring. Since then I've heard pretty much anyone who's anybody has the same invite. Even some of the financial power brokers that most people never meet who fund a lot of the studio's projects will be there."

Caught up in Carol's excitement, Liz said, "All I know for sure is that it's billed as a cross between a fundraiser and a financial strategy session. John told me I need to attend. He manages the money, so I guess he's right. I don't know if he wants me to donate money or time or if it's because some of my investments haven't done so well. I guess I should have asked more. I didn't because I trust John and am intrigued by Mr. Cavanaugh."

"So why not cancel?" Carol asked. "You do so much for them. You don't have to feel compelled to donate if that's what this is."

"Mostly I'm going because it's being hosted by David Cavanaugh of Cavanaugh Corporation." Liz giggled. "He's always been someone I'm curious about. He's so wealthy and mysterious, and..." Liz allowed the word to drag out, making a face at Carol that girls use alone when talking about boys, "...for a man close to seventy, he has the face of a leading man. I want to meet him and see what he's like in person."

"What's so mysterious about him, other than being a filthy rich outdoorsman?"

"When I was younger, I used to see interviews with him on television, and he came across more like a hunter or hiker than a billionaire," Liz mused. "Every time I ask people questions about him, I get more stories that don't fit together. I can't pin down who he is for real. I'm told he's a former jet mechanic, outdoor enthusiast, and he inherited a mid-sized construction company forty years ago from an uncle who died. He took that company, ran with it, and kept making larger buildings. Eventually he was a preferred builder of skyscrapers. Later he took the company into road and bridge construction and finally into large hydroelectric dams."

"Impressive. Do you think he needs a pretty assistant like me?"

"Funny! You're stuck with me," Liz teased, tossing a towel at Carol. "He's done those types of projects all around the world. That doesn't even touch the financial trading and money management his firm does. They say he has a Midas touch. *Time* magazine called him the Richard Branson of the Rockies, and it stuck. That's the stuff that interests me. How can he do it all? Is he as easygoing as they say? Or a self-absorbed jerk like many wealthy people I've met?"

"Wow!" Carol snickered. "I guess that means you are going to the soirée then."

"Yes, of course." Liz giggled. "Hopefully he will touch some of *my* investments with his Midas touch."

"Liz, that sounded naughty. That's not like you."

"I honestly didn't mean it that way at all," Liz said. "He's a very attractive man, but seriously, he's older than my father and not much younger than my grandfather. I truly did mean I'd like some better returns on my money, though. I don't want to be an old actress living alone in an apartment with all my memorabilia and stories of when I was a star."

Carol nodded. "I get it."

"I saw Dave Cavanaugh on some outdoor reality program not too long ago. I don't know why he would do those since he doesn't need the money. He does come across as down to earth and friendly, though, so yes, I'm very curious to meet him. I suspect that's a driving force for why many of the people are attending. If he needs to raise money, I'm even more curious as to why. Who knows? Perhaps it will be fun."

"On a more serious note," Carol said, "well, aside from the soiree, please promise me you'll be careful and stay low key and private on this trip. I have a bad feeling about things."

"Are you still freaked out about that mass shooting in Miami?"

"Yes, and you should be too. You know the woman who does my hair?" Liz nodded. "Her brother was one of the victims. She was out of work for days after the shooting. When she came back, she kept breaking down in tears. Someone else had to finish my hair."

"Bad things happen all over the place; the thing in Miami is terrible. You know I was shot at recently."

"That's exactly it," Carol said. "I don't remember things being this bad when I was younger. It feels different these days, though I can't put my finger on why or how." She squeezed Liz's hand. "Promise me you'll be careful, please."

"I will."

DAVE

The Falcon 7X possessed the speed and comfort few could enjoy for private air travel.

The success Dave enjoyed as a businessman allowed him a wide range of luxuries. For the most part, those things didn't appeal to Dave. The jet was an exception that he thoroughly enjoyed. It was fast and had the ability to get into small airports larger planes couldn't. It blended in fairly well and didn't draw more attention than any other private aircraft.

As he flew to Los Angeles, he reflected on the meeting with his planning and implementation team. The group was somewhat taken aback at first by what he'd suggested. As he monitored some of the breakout meetings, he found some of the people putting up more reasons why it couldn't be done than why it could. In a few cases, they chose to separate out the more negative holdouts and put them on other less important tasks. In some cases, people were ushered out with explanations that their portion of the project had been cut or their work was done. They were paid well and reminded of their non-disclosure contracts.

Soon the tone of the group changed from skepticism to excitement. The mood grew from one of possibility to the actual reality that they would make this happen. Dave's staff was doing a masterful job of winning them over. Each team member gravitated to a different part of the plan they loved or were motivated by. For some, it was a way to take ownership in a growing market. For others, it was a way to win intellectual kudos by doing something that hadn't been done before. Dave even noticed a few people mixed in who appeared excited to finally have a positive approach to prepping. Once the acceptance turned to excitement, the race was on. This could be done.

Dave gave them one month to come back with a working proposal that had the four essential parts. There was a final piece that Dave insisted on that he was convinced were crucial—the community service clause. The communities must be built by people who would give back and invest their time in others and the community. People who would not pull their weight alongside their neighbors in either the minor service or major strategic tasks would not be welcome. This was very important because the plan was to build in community service escalator credits. Those could be used in many ways, including helping some members pay portions of their dues for people who needed financial help and possessed skills the community needed to attract.

Dave expected the initial investors to be from the more affluent set. It was vitally important that everyone involved understand that people like mechanics, farmers, and craftsmen of all types would be the skills most in demand if an apocalyptic collapse ever occurred. Dave wasn't willing to compromise on the community service clause for anyone, figuring it was a slippery slope he dared not begin, even though that clause could drive away the very people he needed to court.

History had a way of repeating itself. If we couldn't learn from the struggles of the early European settlers to America, we would be doomed to repeat their hardships. Had those early settlements brought more people with common skills like hunting, building, and farming, they might have had an easier first few years in the new world.

Dave worried about the wealthy backers he planned to court initially. He didn't mind planning homes of different sizes and levels of luxury, because this was still America. Success *should* earn certain privileges. The point of this community was not to create a socialist commune, but a community of people dedicated to mutual support and similar ideals.

The gathering Dave was travelling to in southern California was the first and the litmus test of what he planned to sell to the investors. This group was probably the most liberal he would face. He chose them specifically because, if he could find at least three solid investors from this group, he was sure he could gain momentum with people more amenable to the endeavor in other parts of the country. Additionally, in this group there were some very public and well-known figures whose participation could mean a lot down the road. Their involvement would go a long way to proving this wasn't just an investment in some hare-brained prepper scheme.

This was a bona fide investment opportunity that was expected to turn a healthy profit in the truest version of America capitalism. There would be nothing shady or underhanded about any of it. The homes would be more modest than what many Americans had become accustomed to yet still modern in most ways with classic styling in a Mayberry-type community. Dave was aware of some gated communities around the country that relied on modern versions of old brownstone homes, Charleston townhomes, or other classic styles, which was a good marketing approach to a gated community. What he was planning would borrow from some of that approach and take it much further. His planned communities would be self-contained and have main streets and businesses that would support both the residents and citizens nearby. They would have drugstores, general stores, hardware stores, grocery stores, and more, like many small towns across America.

The plan was in some instances to have an outlet shopping area or trading post outside of yet still near the community. These retail locations would have to align with the mission or charter of that community. The idea was that if a community produced farmer's markets goods, they could have a place to sell their goods. That idea would work fine before a collapse, but even more so after. If a community trained horses or had a good firearms mail order business, that too could be a source of trade before and after a collapse. The community would charge rent to these businesses. It didn't matter whether it was a mechanics shop, gun store or butcher shop. Some business could be purchased and run by the community as a part of the investments and mutual fund approach of the overall company. While the investment and company ownership portion of this venture had a long list of companies they wanted to own, they would only do it when it could be done at a profit for the shareholders.

The world was becoming more dangerous, fueling Dave's desire to get these communities built sooner rather than later. Among all the domestic issues, there was a news story in which North Korea fired a ballistic recently. A U.S. official confirmed the test failed, and U.S. Pacific Command said the missile did not leave North Korean air space. Dave thought about asking the pilot if the plane was hardened against an EMP then decided against it; he knew the answer.

Although the North Korean missile failed miserably, they would eventually get it working. Iran and Pakistan were helping North Korea. The Chinese and Russians probably were as well to some degree.

A nuclear war or EMP strike may never happen; nonetheless, Dave made a note to have Louis make sure each charter town built a vault-sized Faraday cage underground to protect key electronics. The different locations would need a way to communicate with each other as well as any satellites that could still be reached.

Additionally, small handheld devices like walkie talkies and GPS devices would be worth their weight in gold if an EMP strike ever happened.

He was less concerned about the South Park locations. Some of the old mines went deep and had already undergone massive expansions and support improvements. It would be a simple but costly additional improvement to ensure the storage caverns had some areas set up like Faraday cage vaults.

VINCE

Vince logged in to work remotely from his home office and switched on the news.

One of the perks for working from home was the ability to have a TV running in the background and a kitchen close by. The home was built on a fall-away portion of the land so his basement office had windows to the pool and patio. The pool was green again, and there was a high probability of a dead frog in the strainer. The motor was straining to pull water through. Vince needed to work on it and get the chemicals right and the water clear. That had always been Ellie's thing, and it reminded him of her and Kate. She had loved the pool. It didn't mean as much to Vince, so he neglected to maintain it.

He wouldn't admit it, but aside from the current chaos popping up around the country and in Louisville, he missed going in to the office. There was a social aspect to being there that was good for Vince. He was good at what he did. He understood the technology systems and business plans in a way very few people in the company did. Vince and a handful of people like him had a handle on the pulse of how to keep the ship afloat that some of the people chasing titles didn't care about. It was probably this realization that created the silent divide between people who schmoozed and the people who made things happen. Despite all that, he loved his job and was good at it. He could help and make a difference both for the company and the people they provided a service to. However, more and more his heart was with other things outside of work.

The divorce acted as a wakeup call for Vince. By trying to get his work/life balance more aligned, he was actually better at his job. He rededicated himself to his career and became more socially conscious.

When taking stock of himself and the state of the country, he didn't like what he saw. While he could make personal changes, making a difference in the country was a job for a man like his uncle. Like many people, Vince participated in the political process. He voted every time he could. He listened to talk radio and scoured the internet to read articles that made him feel more educated on the topics and candidates. Yet it was hard to stay involved and passionate about the process. Even the news media folks who were supposed to represent more conservative values leaned the other way. It was difficult not to think they'd become corrupted by the process. Even when the candidates he thought were best won an election, no real ground was taken in getting the country moving in the right direction.

Vince sometimes wondered if the grand experiment, as the country had been called over two hundred years ago, was failing. He was filled with a strong foreboding that America had passed a point of no return and didn't even know it. The debt, the declining and changing public morality, the decay of much of the country's infrastructure, and the corruption in government was not something the people had the will or ability to reverse. With all that in mind, Vince still wasn't one of the people who thought it was likely the country would crash as soon some predicted. As an observer of people, Vince was convinced that most Americans were too accustomed to their air conditioning and cable TV to withstand the discomfort and sacrifice required for change. In more cynical moments, he even wondered whether or not the welfare and comforts weren't all part of some master plan aimed at keeping people too doped up on free stuff to realize they were in a gilded cage. It was frustratingly obvious that the structure that supported the cage was rotting underneath it, yet so many people refused to see it.

America was too fat and too wealthy to fail in just a few years or decades. Without some catastrophe, it would take a perfect storm of smaller events to bring it to its knees. The bottom feeders could feast on the carcass of what the country once was for decades before people would recognize the host had died. By then, it would be too late.

On the upside, Vince would probably never live to see the final death throes of his country. Other than a concern for his daughter or perhaps her children, he supposed he shouldn't care. It was so wasteful when you thought about all that had been accomplished in a little over two hundred years under this grand experiment. As a man, he wanted to do what was in his power to preserve what he could of his country and do what he could for his family's future generations, whether he would be there to see it or not.

It bothered Vince to think that in another generation or two, very few people would be left who would have the skills to survive a societal collapse. He didn't have half the skills his stepfather and mentor had. He knew without any sense of false modesty that few in his family had a fraction of his skills and even less desire to learn them. The skills needed to be prepared or safe were so simple it didn't make sense why more people didn't care to use them, even if merely for a fun pastime. All they needed to do was practice camping, building a fire, gardening, sewing, or canning.

Vince enjoyed being outdoors camping, hunting, and riding horses. He enjoyed it because it made him feel healthy and alive. He loved it because he was practicing traditional skills of his family and his country that would be needed again sometime.

The long, melodious ring of the doorbell chimed. Vince made his way upstairs to the front door, curious who was visiting. Most people called or texted first. Very few stopped by the house unannounced. Most of the friends he had known previously had been more Ellie's than his. Now they were awkward around him and didn't visit much. When Vince opened the front door, Luke from down the street was there. They used to work together and occasionally met for a few drinks after work as casual friends. They never became close friends, primarily because Luke's children were younger than Vince's daughter. Luke was a straight arrow and genuinely good person who always followed the rules. Vince was a gruff, older Army vet who believed the ends justified the means.

"Hi, Vince. How are things?" Luke asked. "I don't think I've stopped by your place in a long time."

"Yep," Vince said skeptically.

"You know where I live a block over in the brown brick two-story? My daughter Jessica goes to North Oldham High like your daughter Kate did," Luke said, still trying to make small talk.

"Nice to see you again, Luke. How can I help you?"

"We're having a community-wide meeting at the old volunteer firehouse tonight. We want everyone to come. I told them I especially wanted to ask you to come."

"Of course I'll come, but why especially me?" Vince asked, genuinely intrigued.

"Well, to be honest, your daughter told some of her friends in the neighborhood about your Special Forces background. With all the looting going on, we think your input could be invaluable."

"I'm sure there must be dozens of people in the neighborhood with military experience."

"There are, though most don't have your experience. I was in the Air Force for four years. Although I don't think most of what I learned there helps prepare me for everything going on right now." Luke gestured to the neighborhood. While there wasn't much chaos to see, they both knew it was close and coming closer.

"What do you mean?" Vince asked. "I know the riots are bad in Louisville, but that's fifteen miles away. There are roadblocks between here and there. We should be fine."

"I guess you haven't heard then." Luke sighed. "We've had maybe a dozen break-ins and home invasions the last few weeks. A few blocks away, a man was killed defending his home in a struggle with an intruder. I heard he was tied up while his wife and daughter were victimized right in front of him, here in our subdivision."

It sounded surreal to Vince to think about all the chaos going on around the country while he and Luke stood on his porch watching the neighbor across the street mow his lawn. "That's horrible!" Vince exclaimed. "It's at times like this that we see the worst of men. I'll be there, although I expect the city should be getting control of this soon."

"I don't know. I hope you're right," Luke answered vaguely. "One of the men in the group has friends in city government. He's telling us the city doesn't know how long it will take. The governor has been hesitant to send in the National Guard. Most people think that's because there is a political rift between the mayor and the governor. I'm also hearing the real reason is that very few National Guardsmen are reporting for duty. Many are opting instead to stay home and protect their homes and families."

"You're right, that does make things a bit more dire. I understand why they wouldn't want to publicize this. Count me in. I'll be there."

Part Five

SOIREE

"The hardest thing to explain is the glaringly evident, which everybody had decided not to see."

- Ayn Rand

LIZ

"Liz, what's with you?" asked Carol. "You aren't usually this nervous. I've seen you in front of press and at premiers and even doing your own stunts all as cool as a cucumber. I've even seen you in a passionate kiss with a leading man even I find attractive and you know I don't even like men that way. So what's got you on edge?"

"I don't know," Liz confessed. "I guess I'm excited about this event tonight. By itself, that's not a big deal. I feel excitement and premonition all rolled into one. I can't really put it into words."

"What do you mean premonition?"

"That's just it," Liz said, wanting to deflect the talk away from Carol's obsession with the mystical. "I don't know. I know this is important for some reason. I can't get the thoughts about this soiree out of my head. Maybe that's because it's hosted by *the* Dave Cavanaugh. I can't help but keep thinking of him as the Richard Branson of the Rockies. Each time that phrase pops into my mind, I want to giggle and feel embarrassed at the same time. It's like I'm star struck or something. It's odd that his fame is totally different from many of the people who will be in the room with him. Do you think he knows that or gets it?"

"You better stop thinking of that nickname because you know you'll accidentally blurt it out in front of him," Carol snickered. "I know I would!"

They were still laughing when Liz's lawyer and agent, John Feinstein, knocked on the doorjamb and walked in. "Liz, we have a few legal documents you'll need to sign before tonight's event."

"Is that normal?" she asked.

"Yes. They're mostly standard non-disclosure agreements. What's different is that the penalties and language are more extreme than I'm used to. Normally I'd say screw it, we don't need this opportunity. The documents are vague and too strict. Yet everyone I talk to thinks this could be something huge. I'm told Mr. Cavanaugh is the ultimate Boy Scout, so you're probably in good hands."

Liz was confused, clearly out of her depth. "John, you're my friend and lawyer, and one of the best in southern California. Don't you have any idea what the big reveal is at the event tonight? Why the dog and pony show?"

John's face got very stern, yet Liz had known him long enough to know when he was using his mock stern face. "First of all, I am *the* best in California, not just *one of* the best." He smirked. "Second of all, no, I don't have any idea what this is about. For that very reason alone, I considered advising you to skip this thing, if for no other reason than I hate how this is making you nervous, and I admire your strength. If it was anyone else other than Dave Cavanaugh, you wouldn't be going. If you said right now you didn't want to go or were having misgivings, I'd be fine with that."

"Would you cancel if you were me?" Liz asked.

John sat down and sighed. "No, if I was in your place, I'd want to meet Dave Cavanaugh as much as I suspect you do. That doesn't even take into account the investment opportunity that's being talked about. Everything that man touches works out well. You're still young and doing fine financially. At thirty, you've still got plenty of years to earn, invest, and save. Still, you could use some of his charmed touch in your portfolio. Money gives you the freedom to pass up roles that aren't good for you or take more time in between jobs to recharge emotionally and artistically."

"You're right, I do want to meet Dave Cavanaugh. I'm truly fascinated by this whole thing, the intrigue and secrecy. The invitation had a teaser about an investment opportunity in some explosive new groundbreaking opportunity. I expect that will be the huge surprise in addition to all the party stuff. Still, I'm sure he knows many people with more assets than I could contribute. What could I possibly offer?"

"Don't sell yourself short. You're a lot better known than you realize. In strict business terms, what you have is face and name recognition. You have a clean and wholesome beauty that speaks to the common man. Don't forget that when you're listening to his spiel. I suspect he needs to appeal to a huge audience at a grassroots level. That's new for him. He's respected up there with the likes of Warren Buffet or Bill Gates for his Midas touch ability to pick and guide an opportunity to riches. He has never needed the masses, even though they love him, probably more than he knows."

"I'm still new to all this. I appreciate your advice, John. The wealth I've earned in such a short period of time is huge compared to what I grew up with; however, I know it's small in comparison to many people in this area. I know I need to invest well and make good choices. Even so, I'm wary of many of the opportunities that get sent my way. Most of them sound too good to be true, like schemes. Perhaps I'm too eager to jump at this thing with Dave Cavanaugh. I've heard too many horror stories of people in this business who were broke as soon as their careers slowed. I don't want to be like that when my career is over."

"That could be true," John advised. "Let's reserve judgement until you figure out what he's proposing. If it's something you should be involved with, we'll make it happen."

"I'll find out tonight!"

"I'll show you where to sign these documents and take care of sending them over to Mr. Cavanaugh's people. Call my cell directly any time if anything sounds fishy or if you just need to talk."

The long drive up the coast from Los Angeles offered Liz time to think. The event was at a gorgeous private country club high above the ocean. It was timed perfectly to see the sun setting over the Pacific Ocean. Liz was glad Carol advised her to take a wrap because the breeze coming in was already chilling.

The soiree was a low key yet still magnificent event. In attendance were perhaps a hundred and fifty southern Californians, a virtual who's who of show business and finance. There were bankers, real estate investors, a few foreign billionaires who now lived in the area, and many of the financial people who backed the studio ventures and managed money for some of the wealthier people involved in the industry. Liz saw several other actors and actresses she'd worked with.

The food and drinks were exquisite, and the crowd was enjoying themselves. The vibe at the event was totally different than many others she'd attended. While she didn't know how he pulled it off, Liz noted the absence of paparazzi in or around the party. Most of the people were relaxing and having a good time like a relaxed social gathering. It was so rare that a group like this could get together and let their hair down without press, paparazzi, or large entourages. When the timing was right, Dave gave a signal to his staff. The bartenders, wait staff, and other service people discreetly exited. Dave's team quietly began circulating and asking the few people who did have members of their entourage with them to ask them to move to another hall for a separate presentation. More than a few of the people became upset about this, and some chose to leave rather than be separated from their people. Liz was alone. She had asked Bill to stay in the car, having full confidence in the security at the event.

Finally, the private room was closed and about a hundred people were left. Dave launched into his presentation, accompanied by stunning pictures of the South Park Valley in Colorado. He was a gifted orator, giving much the same presentation he had to his team in Colorado months earlier. This time, he showed pictures of the amazing progress being made and artist renditions of what the location would be like when it was complete. Dave held the audience enthralled, detailing the structure and how the home ownership and investments would work.

It was at that point he began to see skepticism on the faces of more than a few. Many people were hoping for a get-rich-quick scheme. They wanted to give him a million dollars, hoping a year later he would return five or ten. This wasn't that kind of opportunity. People would have to work and contribute both in their time and money to be a part of this. Dave expected skeptics and critics and forged on, happy that at least the skeptics were paying him the courtesy of continuing to listen.

He decided to alter his agenda some, emphasizing more of the capitalism side of this venture. He didn't want that to be the selling point, yet it didn't hurt to let them know there was profit here too. Dave discussed the types of companies they wanted to build and buy, as well as the profit numbers they expected to make. That was when a few hands shot up.

He called on one man, who said, "The returns are not as high or as fast as some of your other ventures."

Dave nodded. "You're right. I expect with this undertaking the goal is for the company to not only be recession proof, but depression proof as well."

He observed more than half of them looking down at their phones or talking to each other. It *was* Hollywood, and very few comprehended that someday the goose would stop laying golden eggs. It was hard for many of them to grasp that at some point for this country, just as for them, the applause would end and the lights would dim. Many of them didn't realize they were wealthy and well fed only as long as the country continued to operate with such a huge excess that people were willing to squander billions on entertainment. Few of them stopped to think that throughout history this was not common in their profession. Most nations did not spend these huge excesses on entertainment. The system created enormous wealth and a misguided sense of privilege. Dave scanned the faces of those who appeared not to comprehend his message. He wondered if any understood how precarious their position was in the current rare system of financial surplus. The abundance heaped on entertainers was precarious; if the prosperity failed or struggled, they didn't have a plan.

Dave introduced a break in the presentation, allowing the wait staff to come back into the room for fifteen minutes to refill drinks and bring in another round of hors d'oeuvres. After the break, many attendees did not return.

During the second part of the presentation, Dave challenged those that remained. If they didn't feel like it was for them, they could move to the more fun part of the festivities in another area. Dave's team had planned both a Monte Carlo night and a well-known band performing a free outdoor concert on the cliffs with a spectacular view of the sun setting on the Pacific Ocean. Dave purposefully spent a great deal of money to get this year's Super Bowl act to play the event. When he announced the band and the rest of the festivities, most of the remaining hundred people left. That was part of the plan. He didn't want anyone in the last part of the presentation who was not a serious potential investor. If such great entertainment was right outside the doors, only those truly interested would stay.

Dave scanned the room. Twenty-three people remained. "We will only accept investors who will commit to live in the communities for part of the year," he announced. "As residents, you will have to agree to the community service clause."

"I can't decide if you're one of those wacko preppers or a sixties' style hippy trying to build a commune," one of the more uncouth attendees quipped.

The comment was followed by nervous laughter. Dave smiled, stepped down from the podium, and pulled up a chair. By this time, they were all sitting in a rough semi-circle.

"You're partly right," Dave said. "I do have a bit of prepper in me. I'm also a student of history, whether it be the sixties free love period or the Roman withdrawal of the English Isles. One thing that history has taught me is this. Our nation won't stand forever. It was Edward Gibbon who said, '*The five marks of the Roman decaying culture: concern with displaying affluence instead of building wealth; obsession with sex and perversion of sex; art becomes freakish and sensationalistic instead of creative and original; widening disparity between the very rich and very poor; increased demand to live off the state.*' Does any of this sound familiar?"

Dave held up his hand to forestall replies. His question had been rhetorical. "I'm not trying to be an alarmist. Most likely this country will far outlive everyone in this room. However, most of us have families or extended families to think of when we contemplate the future mortality of this nation and our system of government. No other nation in the history of the world has ever lasted in perpetuity. All of them were either crushed from outside or rotted from inside. Why would we think this one will be the first to last forever? As governments go, we aren't young, and by many accounts we're in decline. Almost as many people each year are being turned on to the fact of a potential downfall of this country as are aging into Medicare."

When several people started to speak, Dave held up his hand again. "Despite what some people might think, I'm not a wacko. I don't have any reason to think I need a bug out bag beside me everywhere I go. I'm not advising you to build some bunker to live in with five years' worth of food. What I am saying is this nation could be in decline for months, years, decades, or even centuries. As a betting man, I tend to think we will encounter some type of collapse in years or decades, not centuries. Even so, who knows if or when it will happen? At nearly seventy, I may not see the fall in my lifetime." Dave stared directly at Liz Pendleton, a gorgeous and skilled actress in her early thirties. "But perhaps you will."

It was a powerful and poignant moment. After a moment of dramatic pause, Dave said, "However, this is a moot point because of two things. One, if you believe in an apocalypse or a fall, it's entirely a personal thing, the same as how you propose to survive it is. And two, I will promise you your investment in this endeavor will turn a reliable profit. Additionally, the time you spend each year at your home away from home will rejuvenate you mentally and physically. It will be secure from press and paparazzi. I feel confident that a little community service will give you a refreshed outlook on life that will make you a better person for it. This profit and your increased mental and physical health, not to mention a few fun extra skills, should allay your other concerns."

Liz was enthralled. It sounded perfect. It was not only a reason, but a commitment to get away from the hectic Hollywood lifestyle from time to time. It would be a good place to park some of her money so it could grow. She wanted to be involved and learn more, though at the same time, she was afraid that as a younger person she didn't want to appear too eager or naïve. Still, it was hard to hide her enthusiasm as she approached Dave after his presentation.

DAVE

Walking out with the sounds of the party in full swing echoing in his ears, Dave turned to his favorite sounding board. "Levi, what do you think? How did it go?"

"I don't know these things, Mr. Cavanaugh. I'm more at home in the desert or the woods with a gun in my hand. This country club millionaires thing feels odd to me. What did you hope to accomplish?" Levi countered, dodging the question.

"I'd say the event went about as well as could be expected. I've already poured a lot of my personal wealth into this endeavor. It's important to me that this succeed on a grand scale. If I'm successful on the scale I hope for, then I need to make this type of living and investing fashionable and cool." Dave peeked at Levi with a sideways glance. This was the part of this plan that was most important to him and yet sounded a little silly when spoken out loud.

"Why does that matter?" Levi asked, genuinely confused. "These communities are not huge. You already have all the money you need. These people you met tonight have all the money they need. Why does it matter to you that this becomes huge and fashionable?"

"Levi," Dave started, then paused, struggling to put his thoughts into words. "Every man wants to believe somewhere, somehow, even in a minor way, that he can leave a legacy or change the world during his time on this Earth. Most of us do that through our children, others through work or business. There are a few who can do it through art or science. I even believe there are a precious few leaders who were the right person in the right place at the right time to do it. Think of someone like Alexander the Great, Churchill, or Gandhi. Similarly, there are women like Harriet

Tubman or Golda Meir. Those men and women left a legacy for the world with their leadership. While I don't put myself on a level with any of those great people, I do believe this country has run through its lifecycle of the grand experiment in a scant two hundred and fifty years. That's a short time for a country. We might last ten, fifty, even eighty more years, but we are destined for a fall. With these communities, we can make the skills to survive that fall fashionable. We can help ensure that not only do more people survive, but we can preserve more art, literature, medicine, and general knowledge than has historically happened during times of cataclysmic changes.

"I know this plan can make hundreds of millions of dollars, although I'd be more than happy to see copycat corporations spring up all over. If that happened, we would have made self-reliant communities popular. We would have brought back pride in skills like gardening, sewing, preserving food, building, and farming. People will be much more in touch with the Earth, nature, and each other. We've forgotten as a people that we are at our greatest and most noble when we work together, not only as a community but as a lineage over time. It was once said that if we do great things, it's only because we stand on the shoulders of giants. Do you know what that means?" Dave pressed.

Levi nodded. "I think so."

"I would hazard to say that many people do on the surface, yet few people dwell on the deeper meaning," Dave said with conviction. "It's so important to realize how insignificant one life is by itself. When we cooperate with good people to form a community and we build and plan things that are bigger and take longer than a single lifetime, we are doing good things. Equally as important as doing good, we are fighting the evil of chaos and destruction by building and thriving as a community."

"Makes sense, I suppose I didn't think of it quite that way. I mean, you're not telling me anything new. Although when you sum it all up like that, it does make this whole thing sound more majestic." Levi smiled, wishing more people could see this side of Dave Cavanaugh.

"I've always been careful to invest in such a way that I could get my money back and turn a profit over time," Dave said. "If I decided to end this endeavor at any time, it will still be worthwhile financially. That's my promise to these people. I believe in what Ayn Rand said: '*The man who damns money has obtained it dishonorably; the man who respects it has earned it.*'"

"People trust you. I don't think anyone is worried this is a scam."

"I guess in a way I feel like Noah might have when he was building the ark. I haven't had a vision or spoken to God," Dave responded self-deprecatingly. "Still, I have to imagine that before others knew of the rains and flood, they must have thought Noah was crazy. It was that ark that saved so much of his civilization. It allowed the world the restart the way God intended without the need to start over from the beginning like cave men. Noah had his faith in God to tell him he was doing the right thing despite being ridiculed. I only have my personal faith that what we are doing is right."

"You do know I'm Jewish, right?" Levi chortled, adding a bit of levity to the conversation.

"Yes, but the Noah story is transcendent. Many religions have a story of a great flood. This endeavor needs to come out in the open, and it needs to be accepted on its own merits. If people turn this into a religious thing or too much of a prepper thing, it will be too controversial to be trendy and gain acceptance. They need to start with seeing this as a different way to live and own property that holds a bit of nostalgia and safety in an increasingly unsafe world. They need to earn a profit while participating in something that is wholesome, good, and constructive. The plan is not to have this labeled as a 'prepper' community because that will ultimately drive away investors and bring in only a certain segment of the population. I desperately want a cross section of all types of people. We need all races, economic levels, trades, and skills.

"If I shared all my deepest personal views at this time, it would only bring on unwanted types of news coverage and change the mix of investors and residents. These communities need to accomplish the useful side effect of making people more self-reliant and prepared as a community while creating wealth, safety, and bringing about a renaissance of community involvement and self-reliance."

"That's a tall order, boss."

"Aim for the stars, Levi," Dave quipped. "Then even if you fall short, you still dwell in the heavens. These communities won't survive and thrive without a cross section of skills, people, and views. We need all kinds of people and ideas, not only the people who like to shoot and want to live in a cabin in the woods."

"A cabin in the woods sounds perfect to me," Levi said wistfully.

"Me too. It still may come to that for some of us. Who knows? I'm not denigrating a cabin in the woods. What I'm saying is that when we're separated, hiding, and barely surviving in one of those proverbial cabins in the woods, we're not at our best as a people. These communities are all about us being at our best as a community by combining our strengths and skills."

"Well, boss, I guess I'm starting to understand why you came here first."

Dave nodded and smiled. "Yes. These people would be the first to ridicule the peppers and cabins in the woods people. If they invest, it adds a West Coast legitimacy to the movement I want to create. Moreover, if a few famous and well-thought-of folks get involved, it's a lot easier to sell these communities as something hip, cool, and to be envied."

"You're probably right, Dave. It sounds so different than what people value today. I just don't understand what people want like you do."

"You're right," Dave said. "I don't know for sure that we can be successful in creating a movement that will sweep the nation. I mean to try, though."

Levi grinned. "Then I hope it goes well and they invest heavily and you have beautiful starlets in your communities gardening, riding horses, and shooting guns."

"I'm sure you do," Dave said, "because it will be your job to guard those starlets and make sure they don't fall off those horses or shoot each other with those guns."

"Six months after China pledged to halt cyber espionage against the United States, Beijing's hackers continue to conduct cyber-attacks on government and private networks, the commander of U.S. Cyber Command told Congress.

"Despite a formal pledge made by the Chinese leader in September, 'Cyber operations from China are still targeting and exploiting U.S. government, defense industry, academic, and private computer networks,' the Cybercom chief said in prepared testimony to a House Armed Services subcommittee on Wednesday."

Dave made a mental note to talk with his CIO and determine how safe they were from hackers. They needed to make sure their servers were locked down like Fort Knox. He directed a test on the company's firewalls against cyber-attacks. While this current venture did not provide a service that would be a primary target like an electrical plant, water facility, or military base, all U.S. companies should be put on notice to be wary. It hadn't been that long since a major movie studio was hacked.

He wondered how many other companies had been hacked and didn't know it. Perhaps the hackers or rogue nations were only waiting for the right time to use the data they'd stolen.

VINCE

The meeting at the firehouse in the neighborhood was stressful.

It wasn't something Vince wanted or need at this time. Yet he couldn't back down once he saw the need and was called on. For now, he needed some time to work out the thoughts in his mind, and a drive the Carrollton was the perfect medicine.

It was during one of the neighborhood's many meetings prior to Vince blocking the roads that a home was robbed, the man of the house killed, and his daughter abused. Several neighbors called 911, only to be met with a recording that said all emergency services were overwhelmed, they could either leave a message or go online and fill out a form, and someone would respond when conditions and resources allowed.

One of the women in the neighborhood, a physician's assistant at the hospital not far away, called a private line at work. She was told that the hospital was operating on a skeleton staff and overwhelmed. Ambulance runs were only being done on a priority basis when the National Guard could spare military escorts to accompany it. The neighbors decided to form their own convoy and took the girl and her mother to the hospital. Fortunately, that run had gone without incident.

When his mind started churning too hard, he turned on the radio, which was already tuned to his favorite AM station:

"*...breaking news. Simultaneously at three locations around the city today, officers were ambushed in execution-style shootings. This comes on the heels of two weeks of protests in Louisville related to the two police shootings that garnered national attention, the first being* *the shooting of Edwin Watson, who was pulled over for drunk driving and was shot while lunging for the officer's service revolver. The second shooting occurred during a week of protest when two officers were cut off from support during a march and pelted with bottles. Officer Tanya Johansson fired when she thought she saw a protestor aim a gun at her. No gun was found after the crowd cleared.*

"Since those events, there has been a nightly curfew, and police have stopped responding to non-emergency calls in some of the city's precincts. Louisville is the twelfth major U.S. city to implement a plan for limited emergency services and partial martial law in light of the current national civil unrest. More cities are expected to follow suit.

"Local civil rights leaders have protested that the city is discriminating against low income and predominately black neighborhoods by withholding protection. The mayor and chief of police have scheduled a news conference for later today. We will break in live when that happens."

Vince turned off the radio and switched on his iPod for some music. The news was too depressing. Halfway into the first song, an old one, "Silent Running" by Mike and the Mechanics, he turned it off and rolled down the windows so he could feel the cool evening air and try to relax on his way to Carrollton, deciding he wasn't in the mood for those lyrics.

Part Six

CHANGE

"A society gets the criminals it deserves."

- Val McDermid

Baltimore, MD

Emily Loffler was scared. She was afraid to go to work and afraid to let her kids go to school. Thankfully, school was cancelled for the rest of this week. School officials promised they would reopen next week with extra security and metal detectors. That didn't help Emily. The kids still needed to get *to* school and home safely.

This new round of Baltimore riots was now in its second week. She had already used her sick days and nearly all of her vacation time. Her boss had threatened to fire her if she didn't come in to work Monday. Yet all over Facebook were stories of beatings, carjackings, and personal assaults when people ventured out. It was insane that the city hadn't declared martial law. The only thing public officials would admit was that crime was running higher than normal and some peaceful demonstrations had turned violent.

As a single mom of two, she couldn't share her burden with her ex-husband who'd left years ago. His parents were dead, and her mother lived in Pennsylvania, several hours away. Even though life was a struggle before the chaos, she was proud of her home purchase and the life she was carving out for her children. Now the fear was unbearable, and she didn't know what to do. The desperation of possibly not being able to provide a home, food, and protection for her children was an agony she couldn't describe.

Emily had saved and scrimped for three years for the down payment on the small townhome in the Dundalk neighborhood. It was much better than downtown, and she was proud of her accomplishment. Now she feared she was putting her safety and that of her children at risk to go to work or risk losing her job by staying at home.

She was out of ideas and still nursing a bruise on her face from when groups of demonstrators clashed around her near the subway station on her way home from work two days ago. When she dialed 911, she got a recording. Later she attempted to go to the grocery and the shelves were bare of all the things she was needed. People were fighting over the scraps that she would have bypassed a few days earlier. She came home with only a few cans of pinto beans and several cans of pie filling.

At night, it was all she could do to hold the tears in until the kids fell asleep so they wouldn't see and hear her sobs.

VINCE

Vince pulled up to Carrollton Farm, where he'd hunted rabbits with Greg a few months earlier.

It wasn't as serene at the moment as it had been that morning. Even though he felt bad leaving the neighborhood right now with how things were going, he needed this time away. The further away from a big city he got, the more normal things got. The grocery store shelves were empty in the city. In the country, they still had a few things in stock although they wouldn't last long with many over the road truckers staying home or avoiding dangerous areas. The main difference was the lawlessness that pervaded most of the larger cities' population centers was much less in the rural areas. The more concerning aspect was the fact that cascading effects were spreading from city to city. Events or catastrophes in one city would cause people to riot in another.

The Kentucky Chartertown location was perfect, bordering the Ohio River near Carrollton, Kentucky. Cavanaugh Corp. purchased a huge family-owned orchard and hobby farm. It was surrounded by orchards, fields for crops, and woodlands. The location was about a mile or so west of Carrollton on Highway 42. The site was on the high ground overlooking the Ohio River to the north, with the Little Kentucky River to its east, and it had a deep creek to the west. Included was an existing diner near the blue bridge leading into the actual city of Carrollton. There was a planned marina next to the bridge, just inside the smaller river away from the Ohio in order to avoid the worst of weather and flooding. There were other buildings that could be put to good use on that edge of the property as well.

The plan was to keep much in place operating as it had for years, though they would be adding the gated community on the hill in the middle. It was planned so that it would blend in well to be as unobtrusive as possible.

Surveying the changes since he was last there, Vince saw that some of the ground on the hill where the gated community was being built was already being moved. The bare earth reminded Vince of a skinned knee after a kid falls when bicycling, like a wound on the land. A cluster of people was surrounding Jeff Granger, the construction supervisor and architect from Cavanaugh Corporation. Jeff was busy giving directions, so Vince strolled over to a part of the field that was still untouched and gazed down at the Ohio River. It was a beautiful early spring morning. The mist was rising up from the river so thick the water was obscured below. Soon the sun would burn away the morning mist, and it would be beautiful in a whole other way. Vince liked this time of day. He liked seeing a barge chug its way downriver with only the top half emerging from the mist. He enjoyed the sound of the barge horn as much as he liked the smell of the fresh grass and earth beneath his feet.

"Gorgeous, isn't it?" Jeff had walked up while Vince was deep in thought.

"Yes. I thought you were from Colorado, though. I would think some Kentucky farmland and a river couldn't hold a candle to your Rockies," Vince chuckled.

"I am, and I do dearly love the Rockies, but how can any man who loves nature not look down on that," Jeff pointed to the river cradled between two wooded banks with the mist hanging thick over it, "without experiencing a bit of awe at the skills of our maker?"

Vince grinned. "Well said. And here I thought you were some roughneck construction worker. You have a bit of poet in you."

"I'm no poet, but I do have an appreciation for beauty and a special affinity for nature. I don't have the way with words to explain it like your uncle can. When I was heading out here, Dave told me that the fields, creeks, and rivers of Kentucky have their own kind of working man's beauty. While the Rockies might be the black dress a woman wears out on Saturday night, the Kentucky landscape is the flannel PJs she changes into when she gets home and has her Sunday coffee."

"He does have a way with words, doesn't he?" Vince said with a smile and shake of the head.

"I've spent over twenty years working close to him, and he still amazes me. Speaking of Dave, he wanted to make sure I said hello from him. He also asked me to spend some time and get to know you."

"I'm sure we'll get to know each other well. There's a lot of work to do here."

"There sure is, but it goes faster than you know."

The two men stood in companionable silence, sipping their coffee as the mist burned off and the water became visible. For some men, it was a sign of respect, equality, and companionship to be able to spend time together without the need to speak.

Three more trucks rolled in behind them with more crews, surveyors, and supervisors. As the men unloaded and began their tasks, Jeff and Vince walked away from the river to get to work.

Watching Jeff work, Vince studied him for a moment. It wasn't uncommon for people to be friendly to him in order to curry favor with his uncle. In Jeff's case, he'd probably spent more time with and knew Uncle Dave better than Vince did himself. Vince wasn't so good at the social niceties and was happy that with Jeff he didn't feel he needed to be. Vince wasn't the type to be rude and could turn on the charm when he needed to; he also had a knack for seeing through people. All the fake, pretend stuff grated on him. Jeff was one of the few people who had made it into Uncle Dave's inner circle of trust. That was no small feat. Although Vince and Uncle Dave didn't spend a great deal of time together, his uncle was a great judge of character. While he was gregarious and outgoing in the press and on TV, he was a private person by nature and enjoyed his solitude. If his uncle kept Jeff around as part of his inner circle for over twenty years and spent time with him as a friend as well, then Jeff had to have a wealth of skills and integrity about him.

Uncle Dave had told Vince that he'd selected Jeff as the construction project manager at a national level. Jeff would head up work for several of the community sites in various stages of land acquisition, zoning, legal work, and construction. Dave wanted the Kentucky and Colorado sites up and running first, without delay. They would be the proof of concept both internally to his team and to his early investors as a tangible example of how it all would look and work. After the Colorado South Park location, the Kentucky site was planned to be the most advanced and probably the litmus test for things they would try at other locations.

Dave wanted to begin eliminating the South Park location from discussion. He wanted the general public to focus on other sites and hopefully forget about South Park. It was his preference that they use the Kentucky location as the showpiece. He hoped that if he could make the South Park location fade from memory, it would safeguard the location of some of the more high-profile residents. Colorado and its expanded mines would serve as a major cache location for things that other locations might need in an emergency. It was critical that they start planning for enhanced operational security for that location. The idea was to talk so much about other locations that people didn't even think to ask about the one in Colorado after a while.

"Your uncle wanted me to try and talk you into taking a position with the company again," Jeff said after he rejoined Vince.

"He's made the offer a few times. I respect my uncle as a man and not just because we're family. I'd hate to ruin that by taking his money."

"Think of it this way," Jeff reasoned. "You'd be earning your pay, not taking a handout. If the time comes when these communities are needed, you'll be glad you helped make them happen. This is where you and your friends and family will want to be."

"Right now, my immediate family is less of a concern for this place. They're in Chicago," Vince said, turning his head away.

"You have more friends and family than you realize," Jeff argued earnestly. "Besides, life has a way of looping back around and providing unexpected plot twists. Don't give up so easily."

Vince smiled, realizing Jeff had just given him some of the same advice he had given so many others through the years.

"We all know you can fend for yourself," Jeff said. "You're the type of man who is built from the soul out to defend other people and do good. Taking this job is how you do that best. If the shit hits the fan, you'll be glad you have this as a home base for your family and friends."

"You sound like my uncle, Jeff."

"I've spent a lot of time with him, he's my mentor."

The money would be a good deal more than Vince currently made. His duties would keep him outside an office and near this property a lot. Both things were appealing. He was a proud man. He was proud of the fact that he never leaned on his well-known uncle, did a job that was difficult and stressful, and did it well. More importantly, it was his own accomplishment without any help or patronage.

"Jeff, can you buy me some time?" Vince asked. "What you say makes sense. I'm not ready to leave my current job. I have an emotional investment in what I'm doing. I have people who depend on me there too. I don't want to let my uncle down, and I'd love to spend more time out here." It was hard to hide a tinge of wistful regret in his voice, which didn't go unnoticed by Jeff.

"Okay. Let's change topics, then. I hear things are getting bad in Louisville. You mentioned something about a neighborhood watch group. What's going on with all that?"

"It's crazy." Vince let out a deep breath. "I don't get the why of it and where all the violence is coming from. I mean, I know there was the police shooting and citizens have been manipulated by corrupt leaders into a pseudo race war for years, but this is crazy."

Jeff nodded.

"You know what it reminds me of?" Vince asked.

"What?"

"Do you ever see those celebrations when a sports team wins a championship after a long drought?"

"Yes?"

"When that happens, we see all these stories of people burning their own couches, wrecking their own cars, and ending up in the hospital or jail for no reason at all. It's like some large group psychosis where they get bent on self-destruction and tearing up their own property. And why?"

"I have no idea," Jeff said.

"Me either," Vince admitted. "Still, that's sure what the entire nation feels like to me the last few years. Like different pauses between self-destruction and antagonism against anyone who doesn't think like you. It feels like mass hysteria bubbling below the surface."

"I see what you mean."

"The neighborhood I live in approached me about helping them with a neighborhood watch. Some of them knew about my Special Forces background and thought I could help."

"Smart thinking on their part. I can't think of anyone better," Jeff responded.

"I'm just as replaceable as any other of a million men. Lots of men have done some of the things I've done or been trained the way I have," Vince said in a self-deprecating way, although his training and experience were more than the normal solider experienced. "Anyway, I was glad to help at first."

"At first?" Jeff raised an eyebrow.

"It all turned in to a microcosm of what's going on in the news and Congress and all over the country. Some people wanted to seize power for themselves or be in charge. Mostly it was this one lawyer and a couple of corporate leader types. Some people wanted to set up aid stations and advertise to people to come there for food and other assistance. A different group wanted to pool all the food and supplies in a single location." Vince shook his head. "Those were the people who were least prepared and were running out of things."

Jeff nodded. "That's always the way of it."

"The problem is that all the while, people from the city were sneaking into the neighborhood. They were stealing and hurting people. We had one death early on from a man defending his family. The mother and teenage daughter were brutalized right in front of the father, who was beaten severely and ultimately died. We should have been able to stop it because there were only two ways in and out of an area of four large subdivisions and several hundred homes. I told them I was confident that for the most part the punks wouldn't take the effort to walk in over land and through the woods. We were too disorganized and couldn't tell who was coming and going and who should be there or not."

"That's a hard one. Something tells me you reached a breaking point."

"I guess I did. Last night we had what had to be the tenth meeting at the empty firehouse near the school. I asked them to bring one car per household and be ready for some huge news."

Jeff leaned in. "Really? That would have gotten me curious."

"I asked Luke, one of my neighbors and a coworker, to get everyone settled in. He agreed to go through some of the standard BS and make excuses for me being a few minutes late. After I saw most of the cars crammed into the parking lot and an adjacent field, I parked my own truck in the lot and walked back down the road to the bottom of Highway 1793 and dropped some trees over the road with my chainsaw. It was a spot a little before the road that went through a section with cliffs and woods on both sides. There was no way to get around the blockade. Then I walked back up to where 1793 intersects with a road that goes by Creasy Mahan Park just past the subdivision's entrances, before the old firehouse, and dropped a few more trees over the road there too."

"Smart move, though I'm guessing many of them didn't see it that way," Jeff said, fully enjoying the story now.

"I told them I had one big piece of news and one request, knowing many of them might see it as a demand. I said they could call the law and file an official complaint once police started responding again. Then I told them about the trees I dropped to block us all in there, and if one limb on those trees got cut or moved, I'd find the son of a bitch who did it and make him shovel rocks and dirt over the road ten feet tall at gunpoint."

Hardly able to contain his mirth, Jeff said, "Damn, Vince, you don't play around!"

"They threatened me. I even thought a few of them might charge me. Honestly, I don't know what I would have done if they had. I just stood there and didn't say a word. Then Luke said they should listen to my request, and they could debate after. I told them by that night I expected to see a roster of every able-bodied man inside the barriers between the ages of twenty and sixty to patrol the main roads, the car lot at the old fire house outside the barriers, and homes within the barricades in groups of two in two-hour shifts. I didn't expect all the men to have guns and said they could carry a walkie talkie or a whistle if they preferred. Those men who owned weapons were welcome to carry them. They should also create a rapid response team for emergencies," Vince explained, losing himself in the reverie...

Vince stepped off the chair, and the crowd erupted in chaos. People screamed and yelled and shook their fists.

"How dare he?" a woman shouted.

A man yelled, "You can't get away with this!"

Vince stood there a few moments. Luke was trying to talk to him, but he couldn't hear what he was saying over the bedlam.

After a while, the crowd started to quiet, and one man yelled, "Who cares about your patrol? You won't know who joins or not. We don't have to follow your orders."

"You're taking a big chance if you don't participate," Vince said calmly. "You're banking on the fact that, number one, I won't find out, and number two, society will get back on track soon and you'll have policemen to help protect you from me."

"Big talk," the blustery man said.

"You're right. I don't normally talk this way or make threats. Most of the time I don't care what happens to you and your neighbors. But I will not stand by and see another home invasion, rape, or murder when I know damn well how to stop it. Yes, it's big talk, and I can back it up. Anyone is welcome to try me if they want. Although, before you get angry and do something you'll regret, you need to think about this... If you don't participate in defending this community, you're tacitly condoning the thefts, rapes, murders, and beatings of your neighbors. All you have to give to show that you don't condone it is a few hours of your time every few days. Is that truly so much to ask? If I wasn't the one asking and someone else had brought this up in a better way, would you still be pushing back?"

Vince got the impression they were starting to think, and that was good. "I know you hate me right now. However, this wasn't going to happen if I didn't do it this way. When you calm down, you'll realize that. Most homes still have power. We can share food on a volunteer basis. There are still some places to get food out in the country. I'll help with that. This will make us safer for the time being. As soon as the authorities get control of the city, I'll personally clean up the trees and then you can file charges against me."

The room erupted into a cacophony of voices all speaking at once, although this time they spoke more to each other and in less threatening tones.

When Vince headed toward the door, a woman up front stood. "Surely you don't expect my boys to man the blockade? They're kids and still in school."

"Of course we won't make children pull patrol. Why would you worry we would make them join the neighborhood patrol?" Vince asked her.

"You said anyone over twenty, and they are twenty-two and twenty-five. They're only boys in school. They still live at home with me while they go to college."

After a brief flash of anger, Vince shook his head at the absurdity of it. Finally, without saying a word, he walked out, motioning for Luke to follow him.

"Luke, I'm going to get out of here and check on a project down in Carrollton. I suspect it will be easier to get everyone calmed down if I'm gone."

"Okay, but you are coming back, aren't you?"

"Yes, I'll be back tonight. It might be late, though. My dogs are outside in the yard to protect the house. They won't leave the yard. The invisible fence is powered with solar panels

and should still be hot just in case. Will you do me a favor and check on them and my house periodically?"

"Sure, Vince, but I don't think they'll do your patrol idea. What will you do if you come back and they don't? Surely, you're not going to drag them out of their homes and beat them up. That's rather barbaric, isn't it?" Luke was clearly stressed out and a little incredulous.

"Rape and murder is barbaric," Vince retorted. "Bullying someone into patrolling their neighborhood to prevent those rapes, murders, and thefts is merely an annoyance they can recover from."

"What will you do if they don't participate?" Luke pressed.

"I'll cross that bridge when I come to it. I'd be tempted to leave them to their own fates, although that's not how I'm wired." Impatient to leave, Vince asked, "Would you do me one more favor?"

"Sure."

"Print off a roster with sign-up slots for three overlapping two-man patrols in two-hour segments for the next week. Either circulate it yourself or get a volunteer to do it. Add in a special patrol for the vehicle area near the old firehouse. We'll need to plan for a ready response team for those trained in firearms."

"What if no one signs up?"

"Then when I get back, I'll circulate it myself, and you better believe I'll get some volunteers."

Right then, two men walked out of the hall and volunteered for the patrol. They were neighbors of the family that had been brutalized, and both men had teenage daughters.

"There's your start," Vince said to Luke. "When you and these men go door to door, you'll fill up your roster faster than you expect."

With that, Vince walked to his truck and drove off. A little music and a forty-five-minute drive to the country was exactly what he needed.

A quote from a paper he'd written in college kept churning through his mind that fit this situation. It was Horace who said, "Your own safety is at stake when your neighbor's house is ablaze."

LIZ

Liz had a whirlwind of activities going on around her.

She was very busy most days and would often remind herself when she got stressed out that being this busy was much better than the alternative. Raised in a hard-working blue-collar farming family, she'd been taught to value hard work. Some of her family was skeptical when she announced she was going into acting. It took seeing how steadily she worked and seeing her face on TV and in movies that convinced them what she was doing might actually work out. Her family didn't want her "going all Hollywood," as her grandmother put it.

Her assistant was helping her pack for several trips. "Do I need this much?" Liz exclaimed. "I feel like an elderly matron stuffing steamer trunks for a trans-Atlantic Ocean voyage."

"Liz, you have a lot packed into the next several weeks. You may not be back here for a while," Carol said patiently. "Better to have all this and not need it then need it and not have it. Besides, I'll be there to make sure it all gets where it needs to go. I'll get it unpacked and ready for you."

The first leg of her trip was to Nevada to wrap up filming on a movie she was starring in. While most of the rework had been done on a back lot in Hollywood, it would require about two weeks in the Lake Tahoe area to finish up.

"Don't forget to pack your fun clothes too, Carol. I promised you and the others we would stay an extra week for fun at the casinos and on the lake. I already told John to let the producer know we were going to do that and charge it all back to the studio. The weather is supposed to be good enough to get in some boating and lay out for some rays. I'm sure we can find a few good dance clubs in Reno."

"Fun," Carol said enthusiastically. "Why not remind the studio from time to time how good they have it with you, to keep them on their toes? You could be more of a diva if you chose. You've always been very professional, and you're not known as a difficult star. They should be more than happy to indulge you in an occasional extravagance."

"After Reno, you and others will fly back to Los Angeles for some downtime and to plan for some other upcoming work. I'll fly on to Colorado for a private follow-up meeting with Dave Cavanaugh. I want some one-on-one time to get to know him better. I also wanted to see the South Park location he bragged about. His face lit up when he spoke of it."

"That sounds fun. It should be gorgeous."

"I'm interested to see how onerous the personal activities contribution would be. I don't mind a little hard work. I enjoy getting my hands dirty sometimes. I only want to be sure I won't be required to spend three months a year doing menial tasks while some member of the press could waltz in and snap pictures of me carrying table scraps or cleaning a toilet. I don't want the headache of defending a story that could run saying Liz Pendleton joined some prepper commune or doomsday cult in the mountains."

"I agree. He wouldn't get you into something like that, though, would he?"

"It should be fine. I'll feel better after I check it out, though. When I'm done there, I'll slip into Kentucky and spend some time with my family on the farm. I miss Grandma Jean and my nieces and nephews. I love the downtime and taking walks, riding horses, and even helping with the farm. The time at home and doing those things, being among family and friends, kind of puts what I do for a living in perspective as a bit silly in the grand scheme of life."

"I guess," Carol said speculatively.

"It does for me. The perspective makes the work more fun during the high points and more tolerable during the low points after I go back to the rat race."

After some time back in Los Angeles, Liz would spend five months on location in Chicago doing a made for TV miniseries. Her agent convinced her it was a great role that fit her perfectly, and it would be a shame to turn it down. John's enthusiasm had been contagious, and she'd gotten excited about it and signed the deal. Somewhere between there and here, the excitement had waned.

Moreover, Chicago wasn't the best place to be right now with the utilities failures, union strikes, and soaring crime rate. While crime was rampant in all major U.S. cities, Chicago appeared to be leading the pack, with murders per capita the highest in the nation. Knowing she would be well protected, Liz figured it would probably be fine; still, it was one more thing that took the joy out of this particular project.

The utilities failures, riots, and police shootings had been going on for a while, never failing to cause a problem that somehow extended the shooting schedule. Liz was glad she didn't have any international travel planned. With the new airport security in place and the upgraded terrorist alerts prompted by more frequent bombings in Europe, she would have been uncomfortable travelling outside the country.

She rarely believed the news anymore. She was interested in current events in the U.S. and overseas but rarely bothered to turn on the TV or read online news anymore. The stories that were supposed to be news could have shared the same writing team as her movies. When she watched, it was purely for the entertainment value. Sometimes, though, she couldn't help getting caught up in it. When a story pandered to her way of thinking, she read it avidly. When a story didn't, she called it fake news. It didn't take many cycles of that to make her cynical to the entire process. Sometimes she doubted any of the news was true. Knowing most mainstream news media came through a few finite sources, she hated the thought of being manipulated, so just turned it off and tuned it out.

DAVE

"Dave, hi. It's Jeff."

"Good afternoon, Jeff."

"Hey. Things are going great here at the Carrollton site, but you were right about Vince. He turned down the job offer, although I could swear he wanted to accept."

"I didn't think he'd take it. I needed you to ask, though, and find out for sure." Dave sighed. "I genuinely need him to be a part of this. I know it's his pride speaking. What are your thoughts, Jeff? You spoke with him face to face."

"I think he truly wants to join on a full-time basis. He probably would except for two things."

Dave's curiosity piqued. "What's that?"

"First, to be honest, because you're his uncle." Few people held the confidence and trust with Dave to tell him something like that. *"You're right, that's pride. He doesn't want people thinking he owes his success to influence because of his last name."*

"I get that." Dave sighed. "I may need to talk to him. What's number two?"

"More pride, just of a different sort. While I don't think he has a tremendous amount of love for his job, I do think he's proud of what he does there. He will have a hard time leaving until he feels he has it whipped."

"Hell!" Dave snorted. "You don't whip a job like that. You endure it."

"Yeah. That's the pride coming out. He hasn't decided he can't whip it yet. He's still trying to win. Every small success he has convinces him a win is right around the corner."

Dave saw enough of himself in Vince to understand his feelings. "Keep in touch. Anything you need down there, you've got carte blanche."

"Thanks, boss, we're good here. This is no South Park, but it's gorgeous in a whole other way. You'll be proud of what we have here."

"Thanks again. I look forward to seeing it in person."

Dave hung up with a chortle on the inside. He was as proud of his nephew as if he was his own son. It didn't matter that they went months or even years with minimal contact. When they did speak or get to spend some time together, it was like they had just been around each other yesterday. While he would have preferred to get Vince fully on board, the company would always be there for him. Dave was sure that if push came to shove and he asked personally, Vince would join. He would rather Vince came on his own rather than be coerced.

After the Southern California investors party, Dave had more planned. Others would be easier, because the people were more in his comfort zone. He had already lined up a good deal of the money he needed. Many of the people liked to meet him and would invest because his name was on it and his money invested too. Dave wanted investors who truly understood his vision and wanted to be a part of it. Very few of the enormously wealthy were interested in the personal services part of the contract. They could become difficult when the returns didn't happen as fast as they wanted. Those people he politely detoured to another opportunity with faster returns.

Dave considered Liz Pendleton's upcoming visit, wondering again if it was the right thing to allow her to come to South Park. Liz was a hard person to turn down. In addition to being beautiful, she was very intelligent and possessed a sincerity about her that came through in her roles on film. That gave her an honesty in her performances that most people in Hollywood had lost.

Dave had to laugh at himself. Even an old man could be drawn in by a beautiful woman. He needed to decide how much of the cached supplies and facilities he should show her in the various expanded old mines of the South Park location. Did she only want the charm of a small-town retreat high in the mountains, or was she ready for the whole shebang? Could she handle seeing how truly prepared he planned to be? Would the sight of the cadre of Special Forces men and women training in the mountains alarm her? Dave sighed and decided he would play it by ear. He had a good feeling about her, and he was known to be a superb judge of people.

He also admitted to himself some concern for her safety on this trip. Liz usually flew commercial, and while there were no recent threats toward airplanes in the U.S., a friend had forwarded him part of a leaked intelligence briefing.

Although it was vague and incomplete, it was still enough to make him fearful for Liz and glad he normally flew private jets.

"At this time, there is no credible evidence to support an eminent attack on U.S. domestic air travel, though there is enough chatter to support an increased awareness level. Intelligence gathering efforts have been able to quantify threats in two categories:

The first and least likely of the two threats is a surface-to-air missile triggered from within the United States by terror organizations emboldened by the response generated to the downing of civilian aircrafts in the Ukraine and Asia. This threat is less likely due to the strong controls of those weapons in the U.S. and the difficulty getting them into the country. Analysts recommend enhanced surveillance at shipping ports, especially with containers originating from countries known to support terrorism. Enhanced Security is recommended along the U.S. /Mexico border. Recent transmissions suggest increased communications between terrorist organizations and Mexican drug cartels. Finally, random increased reconnaissance around major U.S. airports will be conducted. Large aircraft are at their most vulnerable to these types of weapons during takeoff and landing. This should be done surreptitiously as to not alarm the American public.

The second and more likely threat is within the airport facilities themselves. Intelligence gathering suggests that many refugees who have immigrated to the U.S. during previous administrations were seeded with sleeper cell terrorists. These people have either trained homegrown Antifa dissidents or have been working to get sensitive work area documentation illegally. While many of these operations aimed at gaining work documentations for airports have been uncovered, the FBI and CIA theorize that many are yet to be found. Although motive is still unclear, analysts suggest that improvised explosive devices could bring down civilian passenger planes, further warning that a concerted effort could have similar impacts to the 9/11 event.

Part Seven

TEAMWORK

"Remember, democracy never lasts long. It soon wastes, exhausts, and murders itself. There never was a democracy yet that did not commit suicide."

-John Adams

Louisville, Kentucky

Steve Billings made it into work. Most of his coworkers chose to dial in remotely. He was a shy, pudgy, bespectacled computer programmer who lived alone, avoided conflict, and liked to read or play computer games. Steve was low on food at home and didn't think the conditions could be that bad. Getting into the parking garage next to the YUM center by 6:30 in the morning, the streets were pretty empty. The drive in from his small home in the highlands went much faster than normal.

Sitting in his cube, he got so engrossed in the e-mails and computer programs he was writing that he forgot all about the riots and crime going on in the city. At lunchtime, he went out for food. Main Street was virtually empty, and the restaurants were closed. Steve walked down to the Fourth Street restaurant and bar area, thinking surely something would be open there.

As he approached Fourth Street, he heard a loud noise like a roar and a commotion. He expected people were either crowding to the few open restaurants or perhaps some protesters were speaking on a bullhorn. The courthouse and government buildings were only a block or two away. Seeing a huge, angry crowd marching down Liberty Street made Steve try to turn away, but they were between him and the office now, and he was hungry. He decided to edge past and try to find a place to eat. He reasoned that they had no cause to be angry with him and he would be safe inside the restaurant.

Steve wasn't sure what set them off. Perhaps he'd bumped someone, didn't fit in, or they were looking for someone to focus their anger on. He only knew he was circled by dozens of angry people. Some seemed from the bad area of downtown while many others just looked like college students. They wouldn't listen to him or let him pass. Steve panicked and tried to push his way through, and that set them off even more. The pain of the first few blows was worse than anything he could have imagined. He went to the ground in a gutter and tried to curl in a ball to protect his face and internal organs. One of the kicks was excruciating, and it felt like something tore loose inside. He could feel the blood in his mouth that reminded him of the taste of a copper penny. Thankfully, he lost consciousness and escaped the torment of pain from dozens of kicks and punches.

Had the crowd listened, they could have heard the man's anguished screams or noticed when they stopped. When they moved on, it would have taken only one person to call an ambulance to save his life from the slow hemorrhage of blood filling his mouth and lungs. It was several hours before a city worker discovered his body.

VINCE

Vince's cell phone rang.

"Hello?"

"Vince, this is Jeff."

"Hi, Jeff. What's up?"

"I'll be back at the Carrollton site on Friday. Can you meet me there?"

"Friday's tough. Will you be there all weekend?"

"I plan to be in town for four or five days. Why?"

"I can't get out there until after lunch on Friday, but if you have time, I'd like to show you around the property the way it was meant to be seen."

"What do you mean?" Jeff asked, somewhat perplexed.

"Do you ride?" Vince asked.

"Pretty much anything. What do you have in mind?"

"Horses."

"I love riding. We have some quarter horses back home in Colorado."

"Then I'm going to spoil you on a nice Tennessee walking horse," Vince snickered. "You'll love it, and you'll experience this property the way it was meant to be."

"Sounds good to me."

"I directed some of the crew to cut a few riding paths in the property and one to the diner along with a hitching rail there so we can grab a bite to eat when we're done. I'd also like to ride some of those buffalo fence lines you all wanted while we're out there, although I don't understand why it needed to be so high and strong."

"I'll show you what we were thinking during the ride. It's not a big deal. We needed to build fence anyway, so why not spend a little extra and give us an extra line of defense if it's ever needed?"

"Well, they aren't totally done yet. The solar panels to power the hot wire on top are on back order with so few over-the-road trucks running."

"That's fine. We'll check out the property and fences and then get a bite to eat. You should also double the solar panel order so we can keep some in reserve whenever they do get here."

Vince and Jeff were getting along well. Jeff shared how much he liked Kentucky and the ark location and found himself enjoying the visits. The entire property was sectioned out in eighths, roughly shaped like pie slices fanning out from the partially built community. From the air, the entire property on the southern bank of the Ohio River might have resembled a half a moon, if the missing half had fallen into the river. It was partitioned off according to planned use. Some fields had been used for certain crops for many years, while others were open for future use. Additionally, the property had a few hundred acres of woodlands and wildlife.

The newly remodeled country diner, which had a view of the rivers and the city of Carrollton proper to the east, was at the base of the hill near the entrance to the property. The diner was doing great business. They served wholesome food, much of which was grown either onsite or by other local farmers. With the augmented space and additional staff Dave had approved, the diner became an instant hit with the locals and was beginning to attract tourists as well. Dave was already talking about turning the concept into a regional or national chain, thinking it would be great to introduce restaurants that used locally sourced meat and produce. It would be a great way to showcase what each community could do. They could share products between locations as well if needed. Creating a restaurant chain that could possibly be expanded outside the communities definitely fit into his idea for the portfolio of businesses that would turn a profit and be owned by Chartertown Corporation.

When they reached the diner, Jeff and Vince tied the horses out back and went inside. While eating, they watched the news on the TV rather absentmindedly, engaging in idle chit chat. Vince suggested to Jeff that he stay on site for the week.

"I'm sure we could get you to the airport and out, although the risk doesn't seem worth it. It's comfortable here, you have a safe, clean place to stay, and with the unpredictability of riots in Louisville right now, it makes the most sense. The police are overwhelmed, and the governor is reluctant to call in the National Guard because in other states that only inflamed the situation. I've been told that many guard members aren't reporting for duty. They're opting to stay home to protect their families and property."

"You're probably right," Jeff conceded. "I need to get home. I have things I need to do, but it's nothing that can't wait. I could do a little fishing or horse riding here if you leave one of the horses."

"I'll do better than that," Vince said enthusiastically. "I'll leave 'em both. We repaired the old stables from the farm and expanded them to be a community asset."

"That's great. Thanks for taking charge and making that happen," Jeff said sincerely.

"I'll enjoy coming out to have another ride this weekend," Vince said. "I need to get away from all that craziness at home and in the city from time to time, so the work is partially self-serving"

"That's probably true," Jeff said. "It sounds like a great addition to the charter town as well. It may end up being part of the charter people agree on for this town when they decide what lifestyle they want to focus on and the people they want to attract."

When the two men walked into the diner, the news was on the TV, but few of the patrons were paying much attention. What struck Vince was that the chaos and civil disruption streaming across the screen had become so common that people had become desensitized to it. It hadn't been long ago that these scenes would have had people paying rapt attention, much the same as they had been during the moon landing or when Kennedy or Reagan was shot. It was amazing how much people could get used to and not even know it.

After their meal, Vince said, "I've got to get the horses back and get to my house. You might remember we set up a perimeter guard, and I dropped some trees to cut off easy travel for the thugs into our area due to some crime we've been having."

"I told your uncle about that. He got as big a laugh about that as I did." Jeff put his left foot in the stirrup and with a bounce swung onto the horse's back with a confidence born from years in the saddle.

"Yeah, it's hard to imagine living in an armed camp thirty miles up the road when it's so peaceful here. Honestly, I think what the nation is going through might blow over. Either way, I think I've permanently burned bridges with most of my neighbors." Vince snorted wryly, glad of the wide trail that allowed the men to continue talking as they rode side by side. "I don't want them to hate me, but I've never been good at *making nice*. It was something I knew in my heart was right. It had to be done. I couldn't have lived with myself if I'd stood by and watched them dither and bicker only to find another family brutalized the next day. Especially when I know how to stop it."

"Sounds like they should appreciate it." Jeff's horse stumbled on a rock, his voice never missing a beat. His balance in the saddle was perfect. "You're right, this stuff shouldn't be acceptable. It may blow over, but it shouldn't fade into memory. This is exactly why we're building these communities. This is where you belong. The neighbors here won't turn on you."

"I guess, but for now I have to get back, do my part, and see this thing through. Who knows? I may need one of Uncle Dave's lawyers when everything is said and done," Vince said as they came out of the woods in sight of the stables.

"Keep one thing in mind, Vince," Jeff counseled.

"What's that?"

"One day, it won't blow over. Maybe this time it will, or even next time or the time after. But one day it won't blow over. What then? What will you do and what will be left for people like your daughter? What will be left for Kate's children?"

Jeff's question was mostly rhetorical and made Vince think. He busied himself undoing the chest strap and girth on the horse. As they washed, brushed, fed, and stabled the horses, they didn't share much small talk, both lost in their own thoughts.

When they were done, Vince shook Jeff's hand. "It was good riding with you. Thanks for the advice, too. You really do sound like my uncle sometimes."

Jeff slapped Vince on the shoulder affectionately, got into his truck, and drove off.

DAVE

Dave was enjoying his visit with Liz Pendleton.

She truly was breathtaking and a joy to be around. Having seen beauty both in people and in nature, he was not easily impressed. He thought of Liz like one of the old-time silver screen beauties, not like the shallow temporary beauty of the flavor the week divas that Hollywood tended to produce lately. Sometimes a rare talent like Liz came along who was able to breathe life into a flat story and create a third dimension with her presence. Liz could suggest a backstory with so much more than words. She could make people believe men would rush off to war and fight through incredible odds for her and had the kind of face to launch a thousand ships. Liz was one of those extremely talented beauties that would be a jewel of the generation if she could stay on track.

What surprised Dave about Liz after spending time with her in person was how real and down to earth she was. In addition to her beauty and charm, she was very intelligent. Dave was impressed with her grip of history and how she instinctively understood his concern with where the world and the country could be headed. She grasped that his plan was more of a legacy Dave wanted to leave behind, not only for his family, but for a group of people willing to follow his plan and take a leap of faith to band together in self-sufficient communities for the common good.

"It's like people don't believe something bad could ever happen. Do they think what we have here is forever? Like some entitlement from God?" Liz shook her head. "Are we the chosen ones, the first country in the history of the world to last forever without corruption, decline, or change?"

"That's exactly what I'm trying to get across!" Dave responded with a childlike enthusiasm. "That's what I'm trying to teach people, not scare them. Think of it like the San Andreas fault in California, only on a shorter time scale."

"I think I follow you. Go on."

"Well, everyone in California knows there will be a major earthquake sometime," Dave explained, gesticulating as he got passionate. "They make buildings earthquake safe and have plans they teach in schools or broadcast on TV. Yet they don't change much about their daily lives or run around scared. They just recognize it as a part of life. Although unlikely today, it will definitely happen sometime. While most Californians don't live in fear every day, they don't ignore it, either. Some of the smarter, more prepared ones may discuss where to go with their children or how to get out of buildings. Some people keep blankets or water in their cars for an emergency or utility outage."

"I totally get what you're saying," Liz said warmly. "That's where my mind was when I heard your plan. In all the doomsday books and movies, people go off and hide for weeks, months, or years until the worst of it blows over. Then society begins again pretty much from scratch. An entire generation of knowledge is lost before we even begin rebuilding. So wasteful!"

"I'm so happy you get it. Although maybe it's the hubris of an old man, I feel this is so important. I need to make it profitable to attract people and investors. Yet if things play out like I expect, money won't be worth anything anyway. If I'm wrong, people get a healthy lifestyle and a good profit."

"I understand. It's like you're trying to jump people past the years of death and devastation in a society-changing event. Your plan could save a good deal of our generation's knowledge."

"Yes, you've summed it up well." Dave grinned. "I should have you do my proposal presentations from now on."

"It's your vision. I don't think anyone could do this better than you," Liz said sincerely. "I'm in. I'm sure I won't be your biggest investor. I'm enthusiastic about the grand plan, though."

"I'm so happy to have you on board. We think along similar lines."

"I like what you said about the mindset of people who built Camelot when they knew the Romans were going to pull back across the English Channel. Surely some of the more visionary people had to have known things would get bad. I wonder if they could have guessed things would collapse into chaos as rapidly as it did, though. Could they conceive that so much would be lost so completely and rapidly in the years after?"

"Very well put," Dave said. "My plan calls for a string of Camelots across the country all working together."

Liz grinned. "Well, if they ever make a movie of it, I'll play the part of Guinevere."

Usually, Dave worried he might come across like a preaching old man when he talked about how communities and people used to help each other and provide aid to the sick and poor. People used to get together to have quilting bees or barn buildings. They loaned each other tools, built sheds, fences, and furniture. They helped watch each other's property and kept an eye on their kids. Talking about these things with someone like Liz was fun. She got it.

Dave and Liz toured various locations of the South Park location, walking arm in arm, their enjoyment deep and genuine. They were so deeply engrossed with each other they didn't notice others around them. The only exception to their obliviousness was the presence of Dave's huge, ever-present protective shadow a few feet behind them. Dave and Liz turned to Levi from time to time for some comment or confirmation or to ask his opinion.

Dave talked about a time when people got together to cook at home and can vegetables, make jelly, or sew clothing. Much of the time people didn't do those things because they were poor; they did it to hang on to valuable skills of previous generations. They did it for the pride of doing something themselves and for the fun of creating something unique. Liz was thoroughly enjoying the conversation and wasn't merely agreeing to be polite, but because she genuinely understood. She interjected comments about her own family and upbringing, and Dave was encouraged to share more of his thoughts, hopes, and plans.

Their talk came so natural and easy that Dave eventually took her to see the mines and show her the vast reserves of supplies deep underground.

Liz was in awe of the immenseness of it all. "My God," she breathed. "Will this community actually consume that much food?"

"No, not unless we are here for a very long time and don't produce our own. In that case, this is merely a place to die comfortably. That's not the plan. This food is here to help others. It could even be for other communities outside our own that fall on tough times. If other people are trying to do the right thing and preserving law and order and morality in a world gone crazy, we want to help them. By doing that, we are helping ourselves."

"So, are you saying you've built the world's largest post-apocalyptic soup kitchen?" Liz teased with a sparkle in her eye.

It was easy for Dave to see why millions fell in love with her on screen. "I guess I never thought of it that way. We always take care of our own first. So yes, maybe it is exactly like you say. Don't tell my other investors, though," he said with his own twinkle in the corner of his eye.

He pointed to the mountains rimming the huge South Park valley. Liz followed his gaze. Off in the distance, she saw huge windmills turning at a brisk pace. "Those are ultra-efficient wind turbines that provide a great deal of power for this charter town," Dave told her. "I always intended for each one to be green, both to lure investors and because those technologies are most sustainable if the SHTF. I expect each community will have a different strength in sustainable energy options. In this location, the wind is constant and strong, leading to a surprising amount of wind energy we can harness. When you couple that with solar options, geothermal and another idea or two I have up my sleeve, this community could be completely energy self-sufficient under several different scenarios."

Liz came across so genuine and into the plan that Dave decided to show her some of the ex-Special Forces men and women who were training in another area. This was the part that Dave was most worried would scare people. He did notice Liz hesitate when she saw them, so he explained that these people were meant to be security for the people and communities and not a private army. They were the leadership cadre of security folks and trainers that would be stationed at each community. Every one of them had met a key criterion in the hiring process; they each wanted to eventually move back home in one of the charter towns near where they were from or wanted to live. Dave didn't want mercenaries. As some of the men and women left for communities that were closer to completion, other ex-military people would be hired and trained for new locations still on the drawing board.

"It makes me feel good that we can find well-paying jobs for these veterans and send them back home to support their friends and family. I'm a strong supporter of our military, both during and after their service to our country, and proud of it. They've given so much for us, it suits my sense of capitalism that I can do this without making it a handout. They get solid high-paying jobs, and they help me secure my investment and turn a profit. It's important to find a way to do things that build, grow, and give back at the same time. It's not that hard if you try. If our friends in government could live by the same principals, this entire endeavor would have never been needed."

Liz shuddered when she reflected how they might need those veterans to make sacrifices similar to what they had overseas here in their own home communities if things got bad.

Later, after Liz left and Dave was in his truck, he reached over to turn on the news, then changed his mind. He'd grown tired of the news. Sports weren't fun anymore, either. He turned on talk radio, and the host, Bill Anderson, was in the middle of a discussion.

"For the actors, actresses, and sports figures to use their platform to pontificate on their perceived injustices doesn't make sense. If the NFL or NBA wants to use their celebrity to preach, let them. However, the federal, state, and local governments should not be subsidizing sports. It's obscene that men making millions get tax breaks when a single mother of three making thirty grand a year can't get a break. The hope is that enough American people will stop watching and buying merchandise to hurt the bottom line of theses sports...

"I call on the professional sports leagues to give up all your tax breaks and subsidies at all levels—federal, state, and local. Give up the stadium deals and tax loopholes and pay taxes like the rest of us. In return, we will make sure our public officials direct at least seventy-five percent of those tax revenues toward an approved social program they choose for the next ten years. Not having tax loopholes and sweetheart deals might mean that a commissioner would make thirty million a year instead of forty. It might mean that an athlete might make twenty million instead of twenty-five."

Bill was called a sellout, racist, and hater for issuing the challenge. What was most interesting was that no one talked seriously about accepting the challenge. Apparently, they enjoyed their protests and notoriety more than they honestly wanted to solve a problem. In a final chapter of insanity on the topic, when some of the few legitimate reporters remaining in the profession questioned these athletes as to what specific change they were asking for, problem they wanted to fix, or what program they would fund, all they got in response were curse words, anger, and shouts of racism.

LIZ

Liz was tired from all the travel and was happy to be home in Kentucky relaxing.

These visits made her feel conflicted. She loved it here, understanding this was the wellspring that replenished her and helped make her successful. While she enjoyed the normalcy of being with her family, Liz also knew she was becoming increasingly acclimated to star treatment. She wasn't ashamed to admit she liked it. Thankfully, Liz was smart and well-grounded enough to keep from crossing any lines to becoming considered hard to work with. It was easy to tell how some people could turn into divas before they even recognized it. Because she didn't want to end up that way, her trips to Kentucky were all that much more important. Sometimes maintaining her values wasn't easy. The road to Hell was paved with good intentions.

"Young lady, your mind is a million miles away," Grandma Jean said as she was cleaning up the kitchen.

Liz snapped out of her reverie. She'd been churning through everything she'd seen and learned regarding Dave's opportunity. She agreed to buy into a home high in the Colorado Mountains. Avoiding the trips home was getting easier when she got busy, partly because as she developed relationships with her friends in show business, she felt justified in planning leisure time with them, too. Her trips away from the business replenished her body and soul. The Colorado location and type of people going there might be exactly what she needed. Liz did feel a pang of regret thinking that, if things truly did hit the fan and she did need to get away, shouldn't she be with her family?

"Grandma, what do you think about all these people who think we're living in the end times or an apocalypse is coming?"

"Honey, it's always something. I wouldn't worry about it."

"So you don't think all this stuff is based on anything? Chaos isn't coming?" Liz asked hopefully. She always trusted Grandma Jean's advice implicitly.

"No, honey. That's not it at all," Grandma Jean said, sitting down at the kitchen table to focus on Liz. "Bad things happen all the time. But good people always rise to the top and overcome. This family is made of strong stuff. If something happens, you'll do well. We're survivors. What I mean is that you can't live your life in fear. You can't live like the end of the world is coming to such an extent that you forget to thrive in the one we have now."

"So, you *do* think something bad is going to happen?" Liz asked in surprise.

"Honey, why are you twisting yourself in knots over this? I can't say something bad will happen or won't. I just know that the world turns and things change. We can't guess what the good Lord has in store for us. Things have always changed throughout history. The peace and prosperity we've experienced in this country is not normal for the world. The good Lord has always given people challenges to overcome. I don't know why He gives us so many trials and evil people to overcome, though. It's not my place to second guess His plan. Things happen, and good people pull together and get through it. They always have and always will. You have to keep your faith. That's just the way of the world. It's good to have friends and family when things aren't going so well."

"I guess that means everything will be okay."

Grandma Jean let out a big belly laugh. Her whole frame shook, her eyes twinkled, and her cheeks got red. "Honey, that certainly does *not* mean everything will be okay. It means that things will happen as a part of the Lord's plan. While I have faith that's good on the whole, sometimes it's not so good for an individual person or the country."

"That sounds terrible," Liz said, surprised Grandma Jean could be so happy with a plan that may mean many of their friends and family could die.

"I suppose it is if you're that person that loses a limb, a life, or a child in service of a larger plan we can't possibly know or understand. That's where faith comes in."

"Then why even try if it's all preordained?"

"Just because the Lord knows what you will do doesn't absolve you of the responsibility to fight for what's right. We have to band together to build and persevere. That's what good people do. Good people build in times of prosperity and preserve in times of struggle. Bad people tear people and communities apart and sow dissension and destruction."

"That sounds like something Dave Cavanaugh would say."

"Think about it from an old woman's point of view," Grandma Jean said. "It wasn't that long ago that we had the Cold War. People were worried about nuclear war. When we had the Cuban missile crisis, people were building bunkers to live in. There is actually a cute Brendan Fraser movie about those times. Before that we had two world wars. My mother told some horrendous stories about the Great Depression. And don't forget, it wasn't too many generations ago we had the Civil War. So think about this; is it possible those events were glancing blows to the United States in terms of hard times? It's like a hurricane that hits a hundred miles away and gets you all wet but you're spared the mass destruction of the center. We've had it pretty good in this country, better than a lot of places. I hope it continues for many generations to come, but you never know. We can't live in fear, though, and forget to enjoy what we have. I figure that's what you're doing in your career."

"What do you mean?"

"You're thriving in the bounty of all the safety and progress we've made in the world. When I was a girl, acting was only beginning to be respected. In my grandmother's time, it was thought of as a low profession. Stage acting or plays have always been a poorly compensated vocation. It's been that way for hundreds of years. Now because of the wealth in this country, we can afford to put you on film to millions of people so they can see your beautiful face making stories come to life. When or where in the history of the world has it ever been possible to do what you do with the amount of pay and respect you receive?"

"I didn't know you thought about my work that way," Liz said, somewhat confused.

"Don't get me wrong, honey. I love what you do. You're one of the best there's ever been. I'm so proud of you I could bust. You need to keep in mind, though, that I have the perspective of an old woman. Everything is temporary, and things always change. We can't get too high and proud of ourselves, or too low. If you were so worried about all the bad things that might happen in the world and you didn't follow your dreams, then what would you be depriving the world of?"

"Grandma Jean, I have some friends I've been talking to. They want me to invest in some projects related to prepping and planning for the future. It's a good moneymaking thing, and it's a good option in case something bad happens. Is that crazy?"

"Well, I don't know about investments, and I'm sure you have people that could give you better advice than me. I suppose some people made a lot of money selling bomb shelters during the Cuban missile crisis. Heck, there was probably someone selling things during the World Wars, the same as people profited during the Civil War. You need to be careful the people you're involved with are of high character, though. Nothing in this world, even safety and security, is worth mortgaging your good name or soul for."

"This is different. This is like investing in companies that build wood stoves and windmills and teach archery and canning as well as other traditional skills that people can enjoy now and still have in case they are needed later. It's like you and your quilting. They will also have housing communities and farms as well, like the orchard and hobby farm up the road."

"Well, I don't know how profitable all that is. I've done most of that stuff all my life and never got rich. If people knew how to do those things, though, they'd be a lot more self-reliant than they are now. Still, my fingers hurt too much anymore to quilt. I do miss it. I would love to teach it to you when we have time. Most of those skills you talk about we've been doing right here for a long time." Grandma Jean's eyes clouded over for a moment, lost in her memories. "If bad things ever do happen, I hope you remember that your home is here. We have our own food and supplies, and you'll be safe." Grandma Jean wrapped Liz in a hug. "As for those communities," she held Liz at arm's length and looked her in the eyes, "I love the farms and the u-pick 'em places with peaches and strawberries, although I don't know if I could live that close to all the other families. It sounds like a cross between a sixties-style commune and some old western fort from the Indian days."

"That's exactly how Mr. Cavanaugh described it." Liz chuckled.

"You mean that good-looking man from TV?" Grandma Jean asked in surprise.

"That's him! You'd like him, Grandma. He's a lot like you, and he is dashing in person."

"Oh, pshaw." Grandma Jean turned to put away some dishes so Liz wouldn't see her blush. "Don't you go teasing me like that, child. I haven't wanted a man since your grandfather died."

"I only said you'd like him is all," Liz said.

"Well, don't you worry about me, honey." Grandma Jean glanced over her shoulder at Liz, the color rising in her cheeks, and asked hesitantly, "So, is he really dashing?"

Part Eight

INDEPENDENCE

"Our constitution was made only for a moral and religious people. It is wholly inadequate to the government of any other."

-John Adams

Chicago, IL

Adnan Khan owned a small shop about halfway between the Miracle Mile and Chicago Midway Airport. He had emigrated from Pakistan in his twenties. When he got his green card at thirty-three, it was the third proudest moment of his life behind the birth of his sons. Life in America was not paved with gold and as easy as people in his home country thought. He worked long hours in a shop he owned below his small apartment that was not much larger than a rich man's closet. He sold everything from t-shirts to potato chips and repaired cell phones as well.

It had been difficult when there were four in the small apartment. Now he was alone, his wife having died a decade earlier from cancer and both his sons moving on with their own lives. Adnan was immensely proud of the college degrees both boys earned after much hard work. They were contributing to the American dream and blending in to this melting pot the right way.

Adnan had seen much violence in his life back in his native country and again living in some of the rougher areas of Chicago. He had experience blending in and avoiding trouble and felt no shame in hiding. Adnan wasn't a fighter. It wasn't that he was a pacifist; it was that he wasn't a strong man and had seen so much fighting and death he knew you couldn't win them all.

The riots sweeping the city were lasting longer than he could remember before. The shop wasn't making any money, so he pulled down the heavy steel shutters and locked up and took two cardboard boxes of junk food up to his small apartment. While he may not eat well or even very healthy, he would not starve. The electricity had been off for a couple days so he could only read by candlelight. Other residents of the building had left days earlier when the power went out. He dared not light a candle for long for fear the rioters would see and try to break in. Adnan saw people ravaged on the streets with little or no police response.

Peeking through a slit in the second floor shutters, Adnan saw a mob of perhaps fifty people on his block. Some were fighting and some were drunk. He was sure many were from the local gang. It wasn't clear if they were fighting with each other or brutalizing a new victim. He heard glass crashing against the building and assumed it was only beer bottles until he heard the *whoosh* of flames that told him it was a Molotov cocktail. Adnan prayed it would go out or the mob would leave before the flames came to his apartment.

His prayers went unanswered. The smoke began filling his tiny apartment. Adnan tried to open to steel shutters to go down the fire escape but had to duck back inside when shots were fired in his direction and pinged off the rising steel shutter. He knelt by the window, desperately gasping for a lungful of fresh air while the thugs howled with glee and drank and shot toward his window. He prayed for the sound of a fire engine or police sirens. He never heard anything more than the crackling flames, the whooshing of smoke, and the laughter of the gang as they fired gunshots at this window before the smoke overtook him and he lost consciousness.

The building burned to the ground. Hours later, a fire engine was dispatched, however, they only had time and resources to spray down the smoldering embers and ensure the fire didn't spread. Adnan's body wouldn't be found for many weeks.

LIZ

Liz and her entourage occupied most of the seats in first class. They were making their final approach in to Chicago for her shoot of the holiday mini-series special.

Sitting next to Liz was her personal assistant Carol. Carol had talked Liz into letting a friend of hers named Jennifer come along as Liz's hair and makeup stylist. Jennifer was young and a little exasperating with her awe of stardom and Hollywood. Her saving grace was that she was very good at what she did. Liz was confident Jennifer would get used to all the glitz and glam in time. She herself hadn't been famous so long that she'd forgotten what it was like to be star struck. She'd insisted Bill take some time off and spend it with his son. Bill would have never accepted if he wasn't strongly missing that father-son time. He assured her that his handpicked replacement, Frank Smith, was an old friend and very good.

Frank was a large, dark-haired, broad-shouldered man with dark eyes. For extra measure, they added a young man who recently left the Marines as back up. He was a tall, sandy blond-haired, blue-eyed man with the physique, face, and square jaw to be in front of the camera instead of protecting her. Frank introduced the young man as Junior. Liz didn't know if that was his given name or a nickname. Things were becoming more and more chaotic around the world. Even though she thought John might be overreacting when he referred to Chicago as Beirut, Liz wasn't about to complain about more security after the events leading up to the awards show earlier this year.

It was unusual for Liz to feel like the older, world-wise person in the group. She was only a little over thirty herself. In this group with Junior Newton the young

Marine, Jennifer, and Carol, who usually acted young despite her age, Liz felt older than her years. Referring to the young Marine as Junior didn't help.

The plane bounced into Midway Field in the chilly wind blowing in from the lake. Chicago citizens were overwhelmed by the number of riots. Tensions between residents and police were high. A number of small explosive devices planted at different water and electrical substations in the Chicago area wreaked havoc, though no terrorist organization claimed responsibility. Experts believed it could be the act of a terrorist group probing the U.S. response times. Others believed it was the act of domestic groups as a part of their protests.

During the drive from the airport to the hotel, Liz tried to make small talk with Frank and Junior. Their eyes were constantly moving and focused on everything except her when they spoke. It wasn't that they were being rude; they were merely very intent on their job, always keeping watch behind her out a window. When they were out of the cars or around people, the men stood on opposite sides of Liz so they could protect her from all angles. When they stopped to unload luggage, Frank and Junior stood between Liz and the crowd. Junior always managed to put himself between her and the bulk of the crowd. They were constantly moving and changing positions to sometimes stand at a ninety-degree angle from each other. She did notice that this kept both men close enough to be in each other's peripheral vision and able to exchange signals while watching the people behind each other's back.

Liz enjoyed this city and agreed to lower her fee for this venture, provided her team had the best of accommodations in Chicago. Since she'd gone through a public breakup with another actor, she wanted some fun time. She'd always said she would never date an actor, but he was very attractive, and they had gotten along for a while. When it ended, she found she didn't miss him.

Furthermore, she thought it might be fun to bring some family up from Kentucky toward the end of the shoot to explore the city with her. She was excited to find her manager was able to get her use of the Waldorf Astoria Penthouse Condo for the entire time. While most of the team would stay in the hotel proper, Liz was thrilled with the penthouse condo. In addition to the hefty fee paid by the studio, she had been asked to allow the real estate agent take some still photos of her in different rooms or on the balcony, which would later be used to show potential buyers of the several thousand-square foot, thirteen million-dollar condo. It was a special level of luxury and pampering above what she hoped for. A few years ago, she would have been a stuttering, awestruck girl at the opulence.

Shooting would start in a few days and probably last longer than planned with the social unrest going on in the city and the reputation of this director. That wouldn't leave Liz much time to shop or enjoy the town. It was St Patrick's Day this weekend, always a special time in Chicago. She enjoyed the festive mood of the city as the rivers and canals turned green with food coloring.

Before they could leave the penthouse for a day of filming, a grim-faced Frank approached Liz, telling her he thought it would be best if she stayed in today. There were shootings near the filming location and not far from the hotel that worried him. Liz was warming up to argue that she didn't want to let anything stop her work, and she was prepared to go to work regardless, when the phone rang. It was the studio calling to tell her that the shoot was cancelled for the day, ending the debate. Liz was still not happy and imagined she could see a bit of triumph in Frank's craggy face.

The hotel arranged to send up catered food at Carol's request. Liz decided to rehearse her lines, then relax on the computer or watch TV. Her mind was still on some things Dave said. The unexpected downtime gave her the opportunity to contemplate things she would miss if the preppers were right and some truly apocalyptic scenario happened. Even though she was swayed by Dave Cavanaugh's plan and agreed to invest in it, she didn't truly believe things would go as badly as some predicted. It was too improbable to contemplate things going that bad for that long on such a huge scale. Perhaps the biggest risk of all was that people couldn't conceive of the need on this scale for that long. Because people didn't think it could happen, they didn't plan. People that didn't have a plan would be the most desperate if things did go south. Liz supposed that was what made Dave's plan so intriguing. It didn't feel like giving up and hiding. It was more akin to weathering a storm on a societal level. At heart, Liz was a fighter and didn't want to give up the trappings of modern civilization. There was too much good in the world not to try and save or protect it.

Perhaps Dave was like Don Quixote, tilting at windmills; then again, maybe so was she. There was a sense of romantic hope in not giving up and fighting for something better and nobler that Liz was drawn to. This grand plan of Dave's wasn't about saving everyone or everything. It was preserving the seeds to rebuild. It was about medicines for diabetics, air conditioning for the elderly, vitamins, and clean drinking water. It was about art, science, and religion and a place where children could get educated and grow up strong so they could be the scientist who cured cancer or to be the man feeding that scientist. This was about all those things that people had been taking for granted for too long.

VINCE

The house was cavernous and quiet. Although Vince was somewhat a loner, this didn't feel right. Without his family, this home reverted to just an empty house.

People weren't meant to be so isolated. That didn't mean he didn't enjoy his times of solitude; he just believed that God built mankind to be in a pack. That was when humans were at their best.

Vince finished talking with Ellie and hung up. He had wanted to talk with Kate, but she was leaving to go out with a group of her friends. Vince only got a moment to say he missed her and was sorry he didn't get to see her more often. Kate quipped that he could send her a new Dooney & Bourke, Kate Spade, or Coach purse and all would be well. Sometimes the things that were funny to Kate tore at his heart.

Kate was a good kid who was well on her way to becoming a great adult. She had been raised with solid moral and ethical values from both sides of her family. Kate had both the advantage as well as the weight of being an only child. She'd been raised in an upper middle-class family in a great neighborhood without exposure to the harsher side of life. She hadn't been around the rougher people Vince had in his life, nor had she spent much time with the blue-collar people of her mother's side. There was much in life and the world Kate hadn't been exposed to and wasn't ready for, no matter what she thought.

She was getting good grades and growing into a beautiful, accomplished woman. It hurt a little that Vince worried that they were drifting apart. As a child who had grown up without much hardship and with access to some of the finer things in life, Kate gravitated more toward the real housewife and debutant lifestyle than more ordinary or practical lifestyle choices. She liked the latest designer skinny jeans or a Mercedes and didn't see anything cool about some of the more traditional values and things her dad espoused. Vince hoped he was overreacting, that it was merely his melancholy at missing her that made him feel this way. When they spent more time together, these things didn't bother him as much.

Vince lingered on the phone with Ellie a little longer than he needed to. He wasn't under any misconception that she wanted him back; he just liked hearing her voice. He wanted to feel that perhaps she didn't hate him so much, even though he probably deserved it. He enjoyed hearing her talk about routine everyday things and could acknowledge that, although he was doing well, he hadn't totally moved on yet.

Ellie talked about Kate's social schedule and her school work. She also mentioned some things about her own life with Malcolm. She shared some of the little things Malcom did to help them get settled into their new life. Eventually the conversation slowed and turned awkward, so Vince made his excuses and hung up.

Vince didn't want to dwell on family stuff and decided this new project for his uncle was a blessing. It occupied a lot of his time outside of his day job and didn't allow him to dwell on things that were over and done. He planned to take some time off from work and spend it at the charter town site in Carrollton. It was a critical time with the Carrollton project. Construction was moving fast, and he was impressed by how well everything was coming together, a little like Camelot without the high turrets.

It was his turn to walk the perimeter of the subdivision with Luke. After the demonstration he made to get patrols agreed to, he definitely couldn't let his neighbors down and not do his part. When Vince got back from Carrollton last night, Luke was excited. Most of the men did what Vince suggested, and Luke asked what Vince would do about the few that didn't.

"Right now, I'm tired of fighting with them. We have enough men to secure the place. If this stuff goes on a few weeks longer, we'll have to deal with them. For right now, let's just do our shift. I'll try to mend fences later."

"Honestly, Vince, from what I saw last night, you're getting a lot more support in the homes behind closed doors than you realize," Luke said.

"What do you mean?"

"Well, outside of a group of hardcore liberals, most of the women support what you did," Luke snickered. Unable to contain his excitement, he kind of danced sideways as he spoke. "I would have thought your approach appealed more to men than women, but I was wrong. The scoop I'm getting is that more than a few men got home after the meeting and caught holy heck from their better halves."

"I guess that makes sense when you think of it," Vince said thoughtfully. "Throughout history, chaos and anarchy has always been much harder on women than men. I don't say that to be a chauvinist; it's a simple fact. We need to work together as couples, the same as we need to as neighbors. We need the other perspectives to balance us. There is wisdom in protecting our homes and families first. It's good to see that people were able to swallow their pride and come to a good decision."

"I never thought about it that way," Luke said. "I was surprised that it was the women who were quicker to recognize the truth in your words about how vulnerable and exposed we were. They were the ones who got past your rough exterior fastest and saw your solution as a good idea. A lot of women are much better at working together as a team than most of these men."

"At least that's a start."

"Don't get me wrong," Luke snickered, "I don't think any of these ladies are going to invite you home for dinner or bake you a cake. However, they do want their families safe and recognize what you did is the best route to that."

"That's all I can ask for, and probably more than I deserve. If this goes on much longer and those men don't have a well-stocked cabin in the woods to hide out in, they better improve their teamwork or listen to their wives more from the get go."

Vince and Luke patrolled the neighborhood, probing the shadows and listening for sounds that didn't belong. Vince was pondering some thoughts related to a television story he saw earlier after his conversation with Ellie. The talking head was droning on about the impact of the attacks on police at three locations around Louisville. The officers had been ambushed by people with assault rifles. The police force was already gutted by several years of budget cuts and early retirements. The quality and volume of recruits wasn't what it had been in previous years, because many policemen knew they were unsupported and always on the verge of being sued.

The riots, civil unrest and general chaos in the city of Louisville followed a pattern seen in many other U.S. cities recently, most notably New York, Denver, and New Orleans. What was of interest and similar in these cases was that some of the same people were arrested in multiple cities during the civil unrest, prompting experts to suspect that some of the unrest was planned by agitators with the financial means to pay for travel and other support. While the belief was that these agitators were part of domestic social change groups, it could not be discounted that the possibility existed they could be foreign sponsored or inspired.

Other cities around the country, such as Chicago, Pittsburgh, Phoenix, and Atlanta, were beginning to experience sympathetic marches for New York, Louisville, and Denver. Certain units of the Kentucky National Guard were being deployed to Louisville. In a rare move of cooperation, the Army chief of staff at the urging of the president agreed to augment the National Guard units with troops from nearby Fort Knox.

Detractors warned that this move would violate the Posse Comitatus Act. A spokesman for the Army insisted it did not violate that Act because a previous administration's presidential order cleared the way for U.S. troops to act in a support role for local police in times of emergency.

DAVE

As an industry leader, Dave tried to stay out of politics. He didn't consider it good for business and had pretty much given up on his belief that people would do the right things regardless of party. Even with that said, he occasionally got drawn into a hot political topic in the course of business or his interviews.

During the flight to Kentucky, Dave agreed to a phone interview about one of his reality programs in which he showed of some of his favorite hiking spots. Somehow the topic swung from outdoors and hiking to immigration. Before Dave could stop himself, he was sharing what he thought was a simple plan. As Dave told the on-air personality, something like this might have been easy to pass forty years ago. Today, no politician would cross the isle and no special interest group was paying for the vote, so it wouldn't happen.

"Some people want a wall built to keep immigrants out. Others want an open-door policy to let them all in. What camp do you fall in, Mr. Cavanaugh?"

"It's pretty simple to me. We need immigrants, but we need immigrants who value our country, ethics, way of life, and want to contribute. People who came into this country by breaking the laws and refusing to learn the language should not be allowed as well as those who don't value our ethics and laws on gender, racial, and religious equity."

"That sounds like a harsh stance. You're forcing people to assimilate. It doesn't much sound like the melting pot."

"Perhaps you're right. However, keep this in mind. I don't think anyone is advocating open borders and taking in everyone. That means we should admit that there already is and should

be a prioritization process and quota. We are merely discussing the mechanics of the priority and quota process.

"That being said, the key word you mentioned is 'melting.' Historically, immigrants came here to melt into our society and become a part of it. Becoming a citizen of the United States should be recognized as an honor for special people and not a privilege or right for everyone in the world. We need to take a strong yet fair stand on those positions and have immigration laws that everyone understands. If we do that, the country would set firm immigration rules about contributing to our country, learning the language, and remaining crime free. There would be immigration quotas each year set by the appropriate department and ratified by the president. The mix of those receiving approval to immigrate to the United States would be based on job research. If we needed twenty percent of the quota to go to the agricultural fields, then those immigrants would be given the opportunity. Perhaps we would need thirty percent for technology or ten percent in medicine. There would be immigration caps set for each field. Studies would be rerun often to see what jobs were going unfilled in the U.S.

"This plan would make it much easier for someone to come to the U.S. on work visas, provided there were jobs going unfilled by American workers. Those people would accrue more points toward a permanent visa by following our laws and rules. Countries that help the U.S. by preventing illegal immigration or by vetting immigrants with background checks would be given preferential treatment in the points for their people toward a prioritization process. Immigrants from those countries would accrue extra points when requesting temporary or permanent visas. By the same token, countries with a bad record of cooperation or a high amount of illegal immigration or crime from their immigrants would get fewer points or opportunities. In the end, the U.S. could continue a long and valuable history of immigration. Immigration could return to a healthy status. That's the way it was originally intended for people who want to help this country grow, not tear it down or change it to be something more like what they left."

"Interesting plan, Mr. Cavanaugh. I'm sure that could ruffle some feathers."

"I'm not a politician. I'm not trying to persuade anyone. Those are my private thoughts. Nevertheless, my plane is due to land soon so I need to cut this short. Feel free to reach out to my assistant for any follow-up questions or information you need."

The Falcon 7X touched down at Bowman Field in Louisville, Kentucky. The trip from Colorado Springs to Louisville was made in only a few hours.

Vince was waiting for his uncle in the parking lot of a small aging airport in one of two black SUVs arranged by Dave's security group. A couple of the men followed Vince through the antique building to greet his uncle on the tarmac. The terminal that separated the plane and tarmac from the parking lot was at least sixty years old and could have passed for a hundred. It was built of red brick with the traditional air tower with a glass air traffic controller enclosure at the top. Vince smiled at seeing his uncle emerge from the plane followed by the hulking figure of his old friend Levi. Close behind was another man he didn't know who carried himself much like Levi. As Vince and two security men approached the plane, an observer would have noticed that they were all dressed casually. They wore jeans and comfortable shirts for the slight chill in the weather that hung loose and untucked in a way that hid their weapons.

In the SUVs, they did have weapons with more punch in case they needed something with more range in the country or more stopping power in the event they encountered an aggressor in body armor. As a weapons enthusiast, Vince chose the heavy barreled version of the FN .308. It was a weapon he was very familiar with and regarded as one of the best made for a wide spread of combat uses. Using his uncle's influence, Vince was able to obtain a couple set up for full auto. That had been no small feat considering how few were made in that configuration and that they were usually reserved for government use. He loved the smooth feel of the trigger and the overall accuracy and fit. Vince normally carried a Winchester SX-AR, sister rifle to the FN .308, and regarded it a reliable old friend in the field. Automatic weapons like these were getting harder to acquire, even with influence. A lot more of the criminals had armor-plated vests and fully automatic weapons than in the past. Having a little more punch in a round made sense.

Most of the city of Louisville was still under martial law. The Bowman Field airport and terminal were protected by the National Guard, augmented by Army personnel from nearby Fort Knox. Only a few years ago, Army personnel would not have been able to assist in this way. On one hand, it was good to see order restored. On the other, Vince couldn't help but think allowing a single person to use the military this way inside the country's borders was like putting a loaded gun in the hands of a toddler. The prohibition of using troops in this manner inside the U.S. was a well-thought-out tradition that dated back to Rome and the legions.

While they waited for Uncle Dave and Levi to descend the steps, Vince surveilled the area to watch for threats or see if anyone was paying special attention to them. Many times, it was a casual bit of misdirection or nonchalance that diffused or avoided a potential issue. When possible, that approach was much more suitable than a display of power. Often, the best way to hide was in plain sight. Halfway between the terminal and the plane, Vince reached out to shake his uncle's hand. Uncle Dave moved past the hand for a hug.

"We're family, Vince. We can hug. No one will think it's unmanly." He had a talent for disarming people and making them smile with a gesture or witticism.

"I'm glad you're here, Uncle Dave. I always enjoy seeing you. We really should get in the cars soon, though."

"Why? Are you expecting trouble?" Dave asked curiously.

"No, nothing specific, it's just that with some of the hate organizations targeting police and the riots in this city, you never know what can pop up. It's better to stay on the move."

"I thought things had gotten better in the city?"

"They have...some." Vince sighed. "It just seems to me like we're always one incident away from it blowing up again. People are treating things like a snowstorm where you stock up on bread and milk and stay indoors a few days."

"And you don't think that's the case?" Dave asked, genuinely interested.

"I don't know. Who am I to predict?" Vince said in exasperation. "It feels more like a whole winter season to me with some hurricanes thrown in to boot. Sure, we might withstand a storm or this week's devastation. But there will be another one behind it. When spring rolls around and the storms abate, we come out and see what's still standing and what needs to be rebuilt."

"That's pretty dire, if you're right," Uncle Dave opined as he was being ushered through the ancient terminal. "I may have launched my ark communities too late."

"First off, Uncle Dave, no one should be listening to me. You know so much more." Vince smiled. "Secondly, I keep hanging on to something you said, that the lifecycle of different entities is never the same. When I say a winter season of change in this country, we all automatically think in terms of four to six months like a regular winter."

"Yes?"

"What if a season of change for a civilization is years or decades? What if the time between storms is months or years?" Vince asked.

Dave patted Vince on the back enthusiastically. "Vince, you're exactly right and wrong at the same time! We *should* be listening to you! I want to reflect on this some, but we need to hope this unrest is just a random summer storm. However, if this time is the beginning of the winter of change in America, then we need to get ready. We don't have to be frantic, because as you pointed out, we could have months or years of good times mixed in during this decline. Still, we do have to move forward with purpose."

"Thanks, Uncle Dave. That means a lot coming from you."

"It's not only your city. Although bad things are happening all over, they aren't getting the press coverage they should."

"That's exactly what I'm trying to say," Vince said. "If five, ten, or fifteen cities have these problems all at once, then the people rioting tend to feed off of each other. A sociologist could explain why, but I'll be darned if I can. I only know it happens."

"Very true." Dave nodded. "It's not only the civil unrest. We can't lose sight of the terrorists and countries like North Vietnam, China, Iran, or Russia. They have to be licking their chops and thinking what a perfect time for a covert cyberwarfare campaign or simple outright terrorism. We're aware those countries sponsor terrorism in our country and around the world; we just can't get the press to report it or people to appreciate the seriousness of it."

"You're right. I can't believe how many people misunderstand cyberwarfare in this day and age. It's like the lottery for aggressive countries."

"Lottery?"

"Think about it this way. Assume that any terrorist organization that is trained and experienced in cyberwarfare has a pre-planned, semi-plausible cover story for any public outcry to their cyber-attacks or incursions. They know their cover story won't hold up to the scrutiny of people like you and me or those in the intelligence community. But it doesn't have to. They have accomplices in the mainstream media that either knowingly or unknowingly help them. They will alibi anything away for the terrorists as long as the cover story meets a political agenda."

"Yes," Dave remarked.

"With all the recent success, they have to know before any cyber battle starts that any cover story they offer will be as good as gold with very little downside. The world, and particularly the U.S., is more than willing to accept any story to avoid escalating tensions or outright war considering all of our problems at home."

"You're right," Dave said, "and it's a chilling thought."

"Those countries and a few other organizations that actively practice cyberattacks view our internal strife as weakness. To them, we are finally vulnerable. That gives them the confidence to continue their cyber assaults on us in a twenty-first century war scenario. They know just by watching TV that most of our media will help them by selling their cover story. That means any money or secrets they steal are a bonus, like lottery winnings."

"I see what you mean, yes."

"It doesn't end there, though!" Vince exclaimed. "Russia and China are very experienced in cyberwarfare. North Korea and Iran are learning and getting better."

Dave nodded. "I have other sources telling me the same thing."

"So here's the clincher," Vince said. "All you have to do is compare cyberwarfare today to traditional warfare and replace the artillery barrage of World War I or II to cyber-battle attacks of today. For a common citizen, that's a stretch. For a military person or historian, they know exactly where I'm going with this."

"I get it. Do enough damage and soften up the enemy, then follow with boots on the ground. If you don't shut down power or weaken the U.S. financially or otherwise, then you merely wait and try again later. We've proven we won't respond and our own people will help support their cover story. It's a win-win for them."

"Exactly." Vince sighed. "Well, we could still right this ship. This is a strong country. We never give up hope."

"Yes, hope for the best and plan for the worst."

The expressway was nearly empty. During the declaration of martial law, cars needed special permission to be on the roads during certain hours. Now that the order had been rescinded, many people who could have been out either still didn't feel safe enough to travel or their cars had been destroyed in the riots.

"This is why I insisted the security detail dress casually," Vince indicated once they were on their way. "They look more like they're going out for a beer and a game of pool rather than providing security. People are mad at the government and police. The criminals are robbing wealthy people. Traveling with men in black suits makes you a target."

"I like it," Dave said. "It's less stuffy and makes them appear more human."

"Normally, there is a very good reason for the uniform. It reinforces that they are part of a larger whole. The intimidation can also resolve some conflicts without the use of force. However, with the attacks on police, it's probably best to slip in and out unnoticed. The city still has curfews to curtail the violence. We're lucky things are a bit more relaxed now. I wish the vehicles weren't so clean and uniform. Next time I'll get them dirty first and not park them together."

"You only need to tell Gus over in French Lick what you want. He'll make it happen," Dave said. "For now, let's go see the community in Carrollton. Outside of the South Park location, this is my poster child for how I want things to be viewed and work."

Vince nodded. "It will take us about forty-five minutes to get there."

"Do you have someplace good in mind for us to eat?"

"If you can hold off forty-five minutes, we can eat at the diner at the community. The food is great, and you'll love the improvements we've made. Besides, Uncle Dave," Vince said with a huge smile, "you're not the most unobtrusive person to get in and out of a restaurant. If I had made plans for someplace private in Louisville, it would still be at least a two-hour affair and not near as safe. Much of Louisville still has riots and crime, the police are barely holding their own, so I think it's best to get out of the city."

The point of Dave's visit was to see the construction site and to press Vince to take a more active role in the project. He wanted Vince to understand his role was crucial. Vince was a natural leader who made good, sound, strategic decisions. At a minimum, Dave wanted to convince Vince to work from home more on his day job so he could be on site for the Carrollton project more. If Vince would agree to that, it would have the additional impact of demonstrating to potential members that it didn't hurt to be further away from the larger cities and population centers. Working remotely was becoming more common. Yet many people still thought they needed to be close enough to work to make the short drive into the office when something came up. He wanted Vince to help prove that regular people could be just as effective working remotely from an hour away as they could from ten minutes away. More importantly, they would be safer and secure away from the cities.

Moreover, Dave wanted to prove how fast he could get a fairly standard but high-end plane like the Falcon 7X from Denver to Louisville. It was one thing to be told how the flight and subsequent drive would work. It was a whole other thing to experience it personally. He still didn't love the idea of needing to go through a larger city like Louisville if things got worse in the country. Louis was checking into airport options in smaller cities like Madison, Indiana. They needed to know how their runways and facilities might handle an aircraft of this size. Still, he was satisfied to see that it had taken less than two hours for this flight.

About an hour later, they entered the diner. Mrs. Bonnie greeted Vince with a hug.

"Howdy, Vince! Where've you been?"

"I'm sorry, Mrs. Bonnie." Vince displayed a warm smile he reserved for a very few people. "With work and all the craziness in Louisville, I got busy and didn't take time to visit. I'm sorry, plus your cooking will make me big as a house."

"Well, you know," Mrs. Bonnie returned a mischievous smile, "a lot of country girls like a big, strong man. A little dad bod don't hurt."

"I'll keep it in mind."

Vince knew Mrs. Bonnie was teasing him, yet it still made him blush. "If you like dad bod, then how do you let Mr. Griggs stay so thin?" he asked.

The Griggs' had been married for over thirty years, and Bonnie had been trying to fatten him up ever since. They seemed like polar opposites both in build and personality, yet it was easy to tell they were deeply in love.

"He frets too much," Mrs. Bonnie sighed. "He's always running and doing, and he's always worried about something or another. You can't keep weight on when you fret so much. That's probably part of your problem. Now look at me. Does it look like I fret?"

"Mrs. Bonnie, you're perfect exactly the way you are," Vince finished with a hug. Dave and the others were standing behind him, watching the exchange. "I want you to meet my uncle Dave. He is the one that financed this whole project and the improvements to the diner."

"I declare! He is a handsome man," Mrs. Bonnie gushed. "And I'm not just saying that because you're the boss. If I wasn't married to Mr. Griggs over there... mmm mmm mmm."

"Well I, uh, I uh," Dave stammered, made all the funnier because Dave Cavanaugh was so seldom at a loss for words.

"Honey, I'm only joshing ya," Mrs. Bonnie said with a deep laugh that was infectious. "I didn't mean nothing by it. I've seen you on TV. It's a pleasure to meet you. I figure you've got to be okay if you're related to this big galoot." Mrs. Bonnie bumped her shoulder into Vince's chest. "Y'all sit wherever you want and tell me what you're in the mood for."

"What's fresh and what do you recommend, Mrs. Bonnie?" Vince asked for the group.

"I've got a batch of fried chicken coming up soon that's better than what you get at that restaurant over near Shelbyville. If you like that, I'll surround it with some mashed potatoes and brown gravy. We also have some green beans straight off the farm here, and I've got some stewed apples made from our own orchards here that came out just right."

"Sounds perfect to me, but you mean the potatoes and chickens don't come from this farm?" Vince asked jokingly.

"No!" Mrs. Bonnie said in mock anger. "The potatoes would be easy to grow if you was to ask them up on the farm to put in a patch for me. Chickens is another matter. It's a little more work to take care of 'em than people know. Then you got all these rules on how you butcher and clean 'em. I would love to have some fresh chickens. I could do it for my own use easy enough at home, though on the other hand for the restaurant we'd have to think it through so as not to get in trouble with the health code officials."

"I'm sure what you have will be great." Vince made a mental note to follow up on the subject later. "I'll bet you have some good pie ready too."

"Of course! You got your choice of chocolate merengue or pecan that's ready right now."

After lunch, Vince took Dave and Levi to the hilltop to go through some of the community's buildings and homes. After that, they borrowed a four-wheeler farm vehicle and took a tour of the orchards and farm fields. Vince made sure to show Uncle Dave the view of the rivers.

Dave asked Vince to ride with him on the way back to the airport. He needed to get back to Denver tonight for a meeting in the morning. Vince was sure he would be pressed to take a larger role. He also knew he would accept because it was so hard to turn down his uncle. He didn't want to let him down.

Part Nine

SURVIVE

"Civilization is like a thin layer of ice upon a deep ocean of chaos and darkness."

- Werner Herzog

New York, NY

Jerome Stevens was eager to march in support of social justice. He had seen a great deal of prejudice in his life and was sure that if he was given an even chance he would have a big corner office like those fat cats in the suits. Instead, he had been wrongly accused and tried several times for small crimes he was sure would have been dropped if his skin color was different or he'd been raised in a different neighborhood. His blood was boiling and passions were high. Eight years of representation in the executive office hadn't changed his life; however, it had revealed the depth of the corruption in government. If the man he voted in couldn't make a difference, then it would take marches and kneeling on national TV and occasionally violent protests to get people to understand what was right.

Brian Mitchel wanted to stand with others in support of an opposing point of view to the social justice group. He wanted hiring, promotions, and pay to be driven by the most qualified person and not by an affirmative action approach based on the color of one's skin or origin. He was experiencing a wave of reverse discrimination in this country and through the mainstream media silencing campaign. He was frustrated that he couldn't speak out without being branded a bigot or some kind of "-ist" or "-phobe."

The two groups clashed. Shouts turned to threats and threats to rocks and fists. Police were monitoring the protest and saw the violence begin to erupt. They were aware of the news cameras so were slow to react for fear of lawsuits and public outcry no matter what they did. When the clash became bloody, the police finally waded in with tear gas and riot gear.

It took too much time. The press of the crowd brought Jerome and Brian together. Bloodied and bruised, they rolled at the feet of the crowd. Other combatants stepped on them and kicked. Jerome was surrounded by people who didn't look like him. He was on his back and Brian was on top. In desperation, he pulled a small nickel-plated .38 revolver and shot three rounds into Brian's chest. Before he could escape from under Brian's body, a tattooed white man plunged a knife into Jerome's side.

The crowd cleared, and the smoke swirled. The last thing Jerome saw were the booted feet of the riot police moving across the plaza. The picture of two dead men locked in a mortal embrace, one white and one black, would be plastered across all the papers by the next morning.

VINCE

Vince was back at the Carrollton location.

It was shaping up well. Several people had already moved in which, strictly speaking, would be against the rules in the future because this site hadn't yet ratified a charter. Still, Cavanaugh Construction was eager to get this site up and running.

The view from the bluff down to the Ohio River was gorgeous. The orchards and fruit fields were vast. The quaint country restaurant was getting great reviews. Right in the middle of that sat a new small town of homes that resembled townhomes of the past as well as southern-style shotgun homes and multi-unit condo dwellings. Along the main streets were small businesses, including a drugstore, a bakery, and a doctor's office, that created a quaint old-fashioned small town atmosphere where people would walk down the street and greet each other personally. The first group of residents was eating it up, and it was easy to tell why. First of all, they were the early adopters and most likely to enjoy this lifestyle. Secondly, it actually turned out even better than planned.

The only downside was the drive into the city where many people worked was close to an hour commute. Most of the new residents worked in Louisville either directly or remotely. Cincinnati was about the same distance, and Vince suspected later they would get more people from there as well. The only problem with attracting more people from Cincinnati was that many of the businesses were on the opposite side of the city, making the commute longer. If they got more people from Cincinnati, they expected it would be the people who telecommuted several days a week.

With the state of things, the corporate leadership expected that telecommuting jobs would take a sharp upswing in the future of business. The proliferation of work-at-home jobs and a real desire for a safe place to live and raise families made the community a real find for many people. With the atmosphere and community culture, it was more attractive, even if the investment opportunity wasn't bundled into the deal.

DAVE

Dave received more current updates from a source in government. He would have liked to have someone in Homeland Security he could reach out to; then again, those people scared even him.

What was scary was that everyone he met in that department was like a zealot. He wasn't sure how the training went, but the outcome was obvious. Dave didn't put it past them to use the IRS, DOJ, or any other three-letter government agency to find a way to wreck not only this venture, but everything he owned and built over the years. It was better to stay off their radar. As a whole, there were fewer and fewer people Dave trusted to view their role in government as a service to the people. If there were strongly ethical people in government, he doubted very few existed after a few years in the job. He was desperate for information yet needed to keep a low profile. It was best to get small bits of information passively, then he could piece things together on his own.

The most common approach in Dave's favor was exploiting these people's greed. The lower government officials were usually planning for their bailout job in the private sector as soon as things didn't go their way. Those people would offer free information to curry favor with Dave. The higher people and those in elected offices were usually trying to get financial contributions or hoping for Dave to use his influence on their behalf. They would give bits and pieces of information as a teaser for the same reason. He evaluated each of these requests against his own strict ethical code. He would help one of these people when it was something he would have done anyway. He didn't mind letting those people think he did it on their behalf to keep the information flowing for a little longer. Dave just didn't trust lifelong government people, didn't regard any of them as long-term resources, and didn't want them to know he cared that much about government doings.

The official word from the government was rosy and portrayed the golden days as being right around the corner if people would only stay the course. The opposing party always predicted the dire consequences of staying on the current course and the need for a change. Like clockwork, every four to eight years American voters did change course, only to be back in the same situation with the party in power entreating the public to trust the plan and the opposing party asking for change. Meanwhile, the nation continued to circle the drain in smaller and shorter cycles of prosperity and chaos.

One source Dave spoke to who knew quite a bit sounded scared. He told more than he should because he wanted out and into a cushy job with Cavanaugh Corp. He told of government austerity measures currently in place, which was no surprise to Dave. What interested Dave most was that government officials, even at mid-level positions, were being advised to move their families out of high risk locales like Chicago, New York City, Los Angeles, and other major metropolitan areas. There were too many bad things looming on the horizon and too few resources to deal with it.

There was a poorly kept government secret that would be career suicide to mention. Over the last twenty years or so, politicians had fostered a mob mentality in each camp. This legitimized their actions in pilfering the public coffers before the next party could gain power and do the same. By radicalizing their parties, corrupting morality, and belittling patriotism, they helped rot the very foundation of what made the country great. They couldn't put the genie back in the bottle. There was very little morality or patriotism left in either camp and no restraint to stop them from taking even more extreme steps. The few ethical people left in government were beginning to be aware that things would get a lot worse before they got better.

What concerned Dave most was how the left in particular dealt in lies both to themselves and their constituents to further their agenda. If they were finally acknowledging truth, even if in a private oblique way, things must be worse than people knew. He would need to accelerate his plan.

To that end, Dave stepped up his provisioning efforts. He wanted to have critical supplies cached in secret bunkers near the various charter town locations. He issued instructions for the certain factories owned by the corporation to ramp up production beyond their order list with the idea that they could warehouse and sell the overage later when or if things improved. The things he wanted produced in higher quantities were solar panels, wind turbines, camping gear, and ammunition.

He made a note to follow up with his people to determine what other items should be stockpiled and prepositioned. This planning brought to mind something General Douglas Macarthur once said: *"I am concerned for the security of our great nation; not so much because of any threat from without, but because of the insidious forces working from within."*

Dave worried about Vince's daughter and ex-wife, who were in Chicago, as well as one of his own most high-profile investors. The riots and chaos were particularly bad there, and he couldn't get an airplane into one of the private airports in Chicago.

When he spoke with Vince on the SAT phone, Vince shared how extremely worried he was for Ellie and Kate. He told Dave he wanted to go up there personally to get them out of the city but didn't want them to think he was crazy if things weren't as bad as the scenes on TV appeared. They decided if the situation didn't get better by the end of the week, Vince would go to Chicago regardless.

The plan was to go in by vehicle, avoiding population clusters, with a couple of special operators as backup. If they decided the mission was a go, Dave insisted they take a low-flying helicopter to French Lick, Indiana, where they would meet up with his old friend Gus. It would shorten the trip, and the vehicles Gus would supply would have more tactical advantages than what Vince had at Carrollton. Additionally, Gus's French Lick location would serve as a forward operating base from Carrollton to support the mission and give them a fallback position. Gus specialized in customizing vehicles for all kinds of pseudo military and recreational uses. With two up-armored 4x4 vehicles, they could make their way into Chicago and hopefully get back out without much action.

LIZ

The landlines in the penthouse and hotel were down, and cell connections were sketchy at best. The outage periods for cell service kept getting longer.

Liz was in Chicago to film at the Navy Pier location, and things weren't going well. The food riots that kept her in the hotel for three days were taking a more aggressive stance. Even with the added security the studio provided at the filming site, they couldn't go to work. Liz and her crew had been holed up in the prestigious downtown hotel for several days. Power, internet, and cable television access had been sporadic. Thankfully, there were backup generators for the lights and mini fridges.

Liz wanted to schedule a private plane out of Chicago, but both Frank and the studio advised against it. Just getting to the small airport would be difficult. If they made it to the airport, there was still a risk; mechanics were suspected of improper repairs or sabotage as a part of their protest.

Most of the studio executives were from large cities and didn't think getting out to the country would be much safer. They advised her to sit still and let things blow over. That was the pattern they had grown to expect from the riots, shootings, and civil unrest. Her security team was doing their best to make sure she had all the comforts of home while they hunkered down. Frank and Junior took turns heading down to the hotel proper for food and supplies.

ELLIE

Ellie had been working from home for an entire week, and it was a godsend. She could earn her paycheck and didn't have to go out among the chaos in the streets.

With the food shortages and riots against police in Chicago, it was for the best. Trying to get to work would have been like running a gauntlet. She was surprised the city hadn't yet instituted martial law. City officials were apparently more afraid of the message it would send to the world than the impact of the murders, rapes, and bedlam. While those officials were experienced at putting a good spin on violent crimes, there was no way to sugarcoat or spin martial law.

Although telecommuting allowed her and others the ability to hunker down and weather another storm of riots, work was still degraded by the frequent interruptions of internet and power. When they lost power or internet access, she lost what she was working on. Sometimes she waited hours for the internet to come back up and then hope her coworkers were on standby to log in and get back on task. Each day, fewer of them logged back in for work.

What was a bit unnerving to Ellie was that usually the periods of anarchy ran their course in a day or two. This current episode was going into day six. It was a partial comfort that Malcolm made it to a bodega early on to stock up on all the eggs, bacon, canned food, and bottled water he could load in the van. The shop owner wasn't sure how much longer he could stay open and reasoned it was better to get paid with the cash Malcolm offered for the goods than to have it stolen by gangs later or go to waste when the power went out again. After that, Malcolm stopped by his dad's old shop to pick up a generator. He planned to alternate it between the kitchen refrigerator and freezer in the basement for long enough to keep what he bought from spoiling.

Recently, Malcolm ran off some sketchy-looking scavengers that banged on the door. It was unclear what they wanted. He thought they were scoping out residences for easy pickings while the police were preoccupied.

To get her mind out of the melancholy mood, Ellie turned on the TV. It was already on the news program, and she let it drone in the background as she worked around the house.

"Chicago police killed a nineteen-year-old man outside a popular nightclub Friday. The man was identified as having an improvised bomb. When confronted by police, the man began chanting pro-Islamic rhetoric, produced a hidden weapon, and shot at police. One officer was injured with non-life-threatening wounds. The suspect was killed at the scene. The man, whose identity has not yet been released by police, was legally working in the U.S. He came to America on a work visa from the Middle East. Experts who investigated the bomb and materials say it's consistent with bombs that the terrorists are taught to make in Middle Eastern training camps. Those same experts postulate that had this bomb exploded when the nightclub was full, we could have expected a death toll of close to a hundred people."

Ellie turned off the TV. The news was always depressing these days.

Part Ten

ADVERSITY

"Nothing in all the world is more dangerous than sincere ignorance and conscientious stupidity."

- Martin Luther King, Jr.

Chicago, IL

Olivia and Mia were totally hyped. They made it closer to downtown than anyone else. A lot of kids were posting videos on social media of the riots and chaos. Tyler had even live streamed a man getting his head crushed with a brick that got millions of internet hits. That was nothing compared to what the girls planned. He'd shot it from inside his second-floor apartment. Olivia and Mia snuck downtown and stayed in the shadows, making it almost to the Miracle Mile shopping area.

"Liv! I'm freaking out," Mia whispered, her chest shaking with excitement.

"Yeah, we're gonna be famous. We might even get our own YouTube channel. We can travel the world making videos."

"OMG, Gucci!" Mia whispered in teen slang, barely able to hide her excitement at actually finding real crime to film. "Focus on those guys. What are they doing?"

"They're beating up another man and taking things from that store."

"Hey, ladies. What's up?" said an older Hispanic voice behind them in a jovial tone. He was flanked by two other men wearing similar colors to the men they'd been filming.

"N-nothing," the girls stammered as they tried to back away.

The two other men flanked them to trap them against the alley wall. The first man, Mateo, grabbed Olivia's cell phone and went through a few of the pictures and messages. "Hmm, live streaming are we? *Hola,* everyone!" he said, aware he was being broadcast across the net.

"Pleeeease!" the girls pleaded through sobs. "Let us go!"

"I think for now I will insist you stay," Mateo said with a sickening smile that revealed some gold teeth and barely hid a sadistic streak. "You promised these people a show. I think we will give them a good one. You have a power cord? I think this will go on a long time." He didn't wait for them to answer. "No matter, my boys will find one."

Olivia and Mia did break the internet. Their screams and torment lasted for days. If law enforcement was watching, the live-streamed video they couldn't find Mateo's gang and the girls. Weeks later, the girls' bodies would be found where the canals flowed out of the city.

VINCE

Vince sat on his large deck watching vehicles travel the road in front of his house.

For several weeks, that wasn't possible. The roadblocks were gone now, and traffic was moving. Although no one came to thank him, no one came with policemen to arrest him either. He was okay with that.

He heard the microwave beep through the open door. Power was back on and the TV worked. Vince didn't think it would last long, so he took advantage of the trucks rolling in to Kroger to buy a cartload of junk food and staples. He wasn't the only one with that idea. The Kroger management hastily created signs limiting the amount a person could spend to fifty dollars per transaction to allow more people to make purchases. Although people didn't riot, it appeared likely a few times. News coverage of similar events in other stores around the city would be entertaining to watch on the evening news.

With things settled down for the moment, the mayor declared the city open for business. Vince ate microwaved Taquitos, relishing real sour cream, a luxury he would miss if things got bad again. He barely listened to the mayor's long, flowery speech about how the different cultures and people of the city had learned so much about each other during the time of strife, had learned to value safety and security as well as each other's differences, and that while the events were tragic, the city would be stronger and more united for having gone through what they had.

Vince was a secret optimist masquerading as a cynic. At times like this, the cynical side won out. He wasn't sure what this whole thing taught them other than civilization was more fragile than most people wanted to admit. They had sadly proven that many citizens were eager for an opportunity to feed the more abhorrent side of their natures.

It was the mayor's announcement that prompted Luke to stop by that day to tell Vince there was meeting with the neighbors to discuss next steps after taking down the barriers. The neighborhood had been upset with Vince and his drastic actions, thinking he'd overreacted. The homes in this choice location near the river a few miles east of Louisville were a target for the hoodlums. Vince's plan had worked despite some vehement opposition. In the end, cooler heads prevailed, and most of the nearly two hundred homes between the blockades had finally been protected.

He finished the Taquitos and went back out on the porch to have a beer and listening to talk radio, the dogs relaxing at his feet. One of his favorite programs was Larry Elder, who on today's show shared a quote by Robert M. Hutchins that reminded Vince of some thoughts that went through his mind when meeting with the neighbors at the firehouse: *"The death of democracy is not likely to be an assassination from ambush. It will be a slow extinction from apathy, indifference, and undernourishment."* Hopefully the events of the last few weeks would snap his neighbors out of their indifference.

People were happy to pretend everything was over and would be fine. They were tired of walking a mile or two to their cars outside the barrier when they needed to go somewhere, tired of travelling in convoys for safety.

Through the period of unrest, some workplaces remained open. While some hired private security, others were considered essential enough to the city that National Guard forces were deployed to protect them. More workplaces had telecommuting contingency plans and technology in place so they could keep getting things done by working remotely, although on a degraded level. Many places just shut down, and people lost pay. Vince found it unreal that the mayor and governor could just issue an announcement that all was okay and everyone would go back to work as if nothing had happened.

One family with a dead husband, a son beaten and traumatized, and a fatherless little girl would always carry the physical and emotional scars from the men who brutalized her and her mom. Their lives would never be the same again. That was nearly two weeks ago and had been the catalyst that drove Vince to create the blockades. How many hundreds of stories like that were repeated around the nation that would permanently scar the country?

The violence finally died down to manageable levels, and order was being reestablished. The governor announced he would dismiss the National Guard tomorrow, and the Army units had already been sent back to Fort Knox. The police came to investigate the shooting from two weeks ago, and the funeral home collected the man's body. It was a gruesome reality that his body had been stored in the basement where it was cooler for so many days until the funeral home could make arrangements for transport. When the group originally took the woman and her daughter to the hospital, they hadn't known what else to do with the body of the father. The funeral home wasn't operating during the martial law period, so the body waited, alone in the man's own basement.

DAVE

Dave met with a group of investors outside of San Antonio. The meeting took place at a luxury resort in the Hill Country area that boasted a great golf course, lazy river, and other amenities.

Something about this group didn't sit well with Dave. He chalked it up to general unease and that people were different all over. Dave was a great judge of people yet sometimes worried he was too picky. There were about forty investors at the Texas location. He was assured that more would follow. In theory, these were Dave's type of people. This was the breadbasket of where he should get his funding.

The Texas site was pre-chosen and paid for by his company months before in anticipation of the need. If a community never moved from the planning stage to reality, the property alone would have escalated in value and turned a profit. This group had more than enough seed capital to get the ball rolling in a big way and were anxious to begin on the charter phase. That wasn't unusual, because the plan was for each community to use their freedom to customize their charter within reason to attract people with similar interests who could live and work together comfortably, the hope being it would make the community pull together better if they shared common interests or goals.

During the course of the presentation, Dave reminded them several times that they would be members and investors and could draft their own charter within the rules and template of the corporation. He believed it was important to remind them that the overall company still held controlling interest in each community.

The corporation could and would use that controlling interest to void any rules in the charter that were unethical or biased in any way. Dave made eye contact with a few of the leaders of the group to emphasize this part of the plan. He didn't want to come across as the heavy, yet it was important they understood the rules from the beginning.

He made arrangements to take some of this group to the Kentucky location for a walkthrough later in the year. The Kentucky location was shaping up to be a showcase location. The town, marina, orchards, and restaurant turned out great. The entire location, with its community buildings and homes, were rounding into form and would show well. That location had the unintended bonus of creating a support community around it as well. It had been well received by local businesses and farmers, providing them with a direct source for crops, animals, and other necessities.

He didn't want to show anyone the South Park Colorado location anymore. That was his home, and while he did like some of the people, he wasn't quite ready to invite them there yet. Additionally, there was the matter of operational security. While these people were well on their way to being major shareholders in the company and knew conceptually there was a charter town in the Colorado mountains, they didn't have the "need to know" more than that.

Dave promised to make arrangements to send a small security team to Texas to protect this location and the equipment sent here for the groundbreaking. Many of the security folks training in Colorado were being deployed around the country to different locations before training was complete. Getting replacements was a slow process, leaving the South Park location thin. The risk was necessary because some of the critical businesses and communities in the middle of construction were not prepared to protect themselves. It was a calculated risk that the South Park location could be protected with a smaller force.

LIZ

Liz was surprised to receive a call from Dave Cavanaugh.

She appreciated having him to talk to about the situation in Chicago. She'd been able to get very few calls through despite repeated efforts to contact her agent, her family, or the studio. She had grown to trust Dave in a short period of time and confided in him like a favorite uncle that had her best interests at heart. She was comforted when he promised to help get her out of the city if things got worse.

After hanging up with Dave, Liz felt more hopeful. Even so, she still wanted to be safely ensconced at the mountain retreat in Colorado, recharging while the world got its sanity back. She worried about her family in Kentucky, even though her concerns were probably unfounded. They came from strong country people who knew how to take care of themselves and could go for weeks without needing much from the city. They would hardly notice the difference.

Liz was aware Dave was building a companion site in Kentucky to the one she'd signed up for in Colorado. She supposed she should have invested at home. In her heart, she always believed that no matter how bad things got, someone would get it fixed in a few days. If she was going to spend some time on an extended vacation while society went through its tantrums for a few weeks, then what better location than a pristine Colorado mountaintop town?

Liz shared those exact thoughts on the phone with Dave. At the time, she hadn't noticed Dave didn't respond; he'd just moved on to the next topic and promised to have someone check on her family. He emphasized that as a member of the extended charter town family, she could always come to him. He cared about her, and they looked out for each other.

Part Eleven

CHAOS

"There are two spiritual dangers in not owning a farm. One is the danger of supposing that breakfast comes from the grocery, and the other that heat comes from the furnace."

- Aldo Leopold

VINCE

Usually Vince texted Kate. He preferred hearing her voice but got more frequent contact with her when texting. When they did talk on the phone, the conversations soon devolved into awkward silences. He missed when she was younger and talking to her was so natural. Vince wanted her to know how terribly much he missed her yet didn't want to drive her away with uncomfortable emotional pressure.

With the riots going still going on strong in Chicago, Vince decided to call while he was at Carrollton. Kate was a strong-willed person with plans to become a lawyer. As strong and determined as she was, when Vince spoke to her, he detected that underneath she was worried and a little scared. Having self-doubt was not something Kate was used to. The reality of the riots and chaos was different and not something most people were prepared for.

"Dad, I'm going stir crazy because Mom and Malcolm won't let me go anywhere except next door."

"They're trying to keep you safe, hon."

"My friends are posting some of the craziness around the city on social media sites. They're seeing it firsthand and taking pictures."

This terrified Vince. It was ominous to hear that some of Kate's friends hadn't posted anything after going out to see the chaos in person. "Hon, you have no idea how dangerous that is," Vince said, more sharply than he intended.

"You might be right, but this is history. In twenty years I don't want to say I stayed home

when everyone I know saw history in person, like Tiananmen Square or the hippies at the National Mall," Kate responded.

"Kate..."

"By the way, Malcolm ran off some looters that banged on our doors and windows."

None of this helped allay Vince's fear for their safety. Still, he forced himself to remain calm and reassuring for Kate's benefit.

Driving curvy country roads was relaxing for Vince. He'd left the Carrollton location a few minutes ago and was trying to find a family farm owned by the Pendletons. He'd driven these roads many times and hunted this area and never would have guessed these folks were related to the famous actress. Uncle Dave asked him to talk to the family and assure them she was safe, and if it was necessary they would send a team in to bring her home.

After finding the place and meeting them, they were as down to Earth as anyone else in the area. As a matter of fact, a couple of them seemed familiar. He might have known them from a casual conversation at a feed store or perhaps one of the music nights at the local winery called Smith-Berry.

The matron of the family, Grandma Jean, told him they were worried sick about Liz up there in Chicago. Vince assured her that his uncle had talked to Liz and that she was safe in the penthouse at the Waldorf Astoria. They tried calling her again while he was there but couldn't get through. The family was concerned that she wouldn't be able to tell them if things got worse and she needed help.

"Rest assured," Vince said, "my uncle is working on a way to get her a SAT phone. As soon as he does, I'll make sure to tell you. If your land line or cell phones aren't working, I'll come bring you a phone too."

Vince's assurances gave them a level of comfort. What they couldn't know was that it added a level of stress for Vince. It was another group of people he now felt responsible for. At heart, Vince was a protector. Although these people didn't truly need it, it was in his nature to feel a sense of responsibility for people he liked and cared about. He supposed that was why he could be so standoffish to people at times, as an emotional self-defense. It wasn't in him to not to try and help people he cared for or liked. The secret kryptonite for Vince was that he liked a lot of people who had no idea he did.

The Pendletons expressed no real concerns for themselves other than that their beef cattle and corn crops were not moving to market. The markets in Louisville and Cincinnati were closed, and it wasn't safe to take cattle or corn to the cities anyway.

Knowing his uncle was gathering food, Vince offered to buy a good deal of what they had to fill some of the supply bunkers. Before he could take delivery, he needed to ensure the charter town had enough storage for the corn and refrigeration for the beef. He planned to double check that they could secure an option to get the beef butchered. Vince made a note to himself to reach out to some of the local deer processors, feeling sure they'd appreciate the work in barter or trade for their services and be glad to help.

"I'll check with Uncle Dave to see if he thinks it makes sense to buy more of the crops and beef for other locations. Shipping problems may slow things down."

The Pendletons thanked him profusely. Vince was happy that this had turned out to be a good visit all the way around. He'd found a good source of beef and corn close to the charter town. Additionally, he met some good salt of the earth people that he got along with well.

As Vince left the Pendleton farm, he was able to get some text messages through to Kate. He was so glad at seeing her reply he pulled over to call her immediately, expressing his joy that she was safe. Kate sounded scared but was handling it well. Vince told her that he would be there for her the moment they were ready.

"I promise you, hon, I'll move Heaven and Earth to keep you safe, and your mom too."

"I don't think that's necessary yet," Kate said, sounding a lot like her mom. *"You never know what tomorrow will bring, though."*

DAVE

Dave hung up the phone with a smile.

He'd instructed Louis to work with Vince to make arrangements to buy the beef and corn from the Pendletons. Dave fully understood the value of supporting the American farmer and especially one close to home.

His mind began to churn immediately when Vince first shared the Pendleton information. When things returned to normal, he was aware of some organic restaurant chains he could route the excess products to. If things stayed bad or got worse, he could redirect that food to his communities. In return, his people would provide protection for the Pendletons as much as possible. Dave always hoped some of the communities would have a more agrarian charter, thinking those would be much needed skills if things truly went bad.

The American farmer wasn't as venerated as in the past. That was a shame, considering how important their role was for the country and the world. The community in Texas was working on a charter that included a huge old fashioned Texas ranch around the community. As good as that was, Dave was convinced he needed more. The Texas cattle were longhorns; the Pendletons raised a variation of Black Angus. While longhorns were some of the hardiest brutes on the planet, many people, including Dave, preferred the taste of Angus. It made sense to invest in Angus cattle that would be in high demand for the organic restaurants. For the long term, Dave preferred not to have all his eggs in one basket. He was excited about the Texas community and fully supported what they wanted to do. On the other hand, he couldn't help feeling some discomfort at the thought that he might be propping up a post-apocalypse Texas land baron. It was essential that the community have the right leadership. They needed to have a strong moral foundation and sense of justice.

Dave instructed his personal assistant, Louis Clark, to request a small change to the charter town project. This change would create a division head whose responsibility would be to launch an organic foods distribution network as a subsidiary of the Chartertown Corporation. The organic foods division would be invested in and take its direction from board members on the Chartertown mutual fund investment arm of the venture. That division leader would be instructed to search out and foster other such ventures within or around other charter town communities. Dave hoped this would incent more farming and produce to be grown around the charter towns. This process should turn a profit and encourage other communities to become food suppliers as a part of their charter. It would bring money back into their community and help make them more self-sustaining at a local level. Seeing the success and feedback might spur them to over-produce for other communities and incent more agrarian pursuits either as a community hobby or business.

Dave had another motive for supporting this idea. He openly pushed for reduced fees for people with critical skill sets. Even so, he didn't think most investors stopped to consider much about what that meant. The few people who did question that clause assumed it meant people like doctors, teachers, mechanics, and solar panel repair people would join. While that was all true, what they didn't know was that Dave wanted crop workers and farmers, hunters, and carpenters to join as well. And he wanted those farmers and cattle workers to start out on a more even footing and not be viewed as charity cases.

While Dave was talking to Louis, he also sent instructions to other leaders to get the word out that he would be offering bonuses for any construction workers that made it to work during the crisis. While he didn't believe the current crisis was the one that wouldn't end, you never knew.

When he was done with those instructions, he changed gears to call Gus in French Lick. It was important he get a heads up that Vince and the team might need him. Dave arranged for Gus to get working on a few up-armored all-terrain vehicles for each of the communities with the understanding that Vince may need a couple of them sooner rather than later. "And Gus, don't make 'em so clean and pretty this time," he remembered to add with a chuckle.

Gus had a few large, well-hidden underground fuel tanks. Dave asked how full they were and if he would be open to lease a couple of them to the charter town for backup of fuel storage. It was always good to diversify and have contingency plans in places that were not obvious.

Dave was getting settled into the South Park Colorado location. Being up here made the rest of the world seem a million miles away, and since the onset of the national crisis, it was even more so. The South Park valley had more than one small town. He usually stopped in Fairplay for supplies or lunch at the diner. He enjoyed relaxing and chatting with the locals. His favorite watering hole and restaurant was unpretentiously called the South Park Steakhouse. In the valley, stores were open, schools were in session, and people went to church on Sunday. Still, Dave knew this valley wasn't totally self-sufficient. Sooner or later the strife in the cities would impact life up here. So far, they had been untouched by the turmoil and violence down in the big cities. People here acted oblivious to what was going on in the rest of country. It wasn't that they didn't know; it was that they mostly didn't care. Most of them always assumed something like this would happen anyway. People opened stores and conducted business, and the cattle ranches went about their business much as they had for a hundred years or more.

Inside the valley, and especially the town of Fairplay, life still went on with a peaceful small-town feel. Power was plentiful and coming in strong from multiple sources. Due to the Renewable Energy initiative passed by the Colorado voters more than a decade ago, wind energy sources had been on a steady uptick in the state. Dave made sure the South Park valley was one of the leading experimental sites for that effort. The valley was perfectly situated to take advantage of the winds over the mountains that made use of the huge, efficient wind turbines. That effort, combined with abundant solar energy and the natural gas facility still producing, meant that things hadn't changed much in the valley. While it wasn't always warm in South Park, the sun did shine on the mountains so the solar power grid ran at peak capacity.

If Dave hadn't loved this valley for its beauty and people, he would have loved it for the perfect location it was for the central Ark of America. This was a place to store the seeds of rebirth for the country. This valley would be an ark of art, humanity, medicine, religion, and people in the face of tough times to come.

There were only a handful of roads that someone could use to get into the valley. They could stop most of the traffic to and from the valley by blocking two of the main routes at certain places. The other routes were not well known to people who weren't locals and weren't accessible most of the year if you didn't have a four-wheel drive and snow chains.

The most commonly traveled two-lane highway traversed a gorge for a dozen miles before reaching the valley. Dave arranged for some of his security people to dress as road workers and block the bridge under the guise of dangerous conditions. They would only let people through who were locals or bringing in supplies, turning away those who didn't have a reason to be here. Admittedly, it was a bit heavy-handed, and if the people that lived in the valley knew what he was doing, they might turn against him. They were a proud and independent group. Dave only expected to do it for a short period of time. If things got better, he would pull his people back and no one would be the wiser. If things didn't improve, he would go to the valley council and admit what he'd done in an effort to gain their support. Because the other roads were lightly traveled and not well known, Dave arranged for roving teams to monitor those roads. They were instructed not to take any action yet.

He didn't harbor the romantic feelings of many in the prepper community of one man against the world. He just believed in being prepared at a grander community level from the beginning. The only purpose of bugging out and bunkering in away from the world would be to weather an initial storm of chaos. There was so much good in the world they owed it to the next generation to ensure it wasn't lost in the flames of change. While Dave's charter town version of a bunker was fabulous, his plan was for naught if it didn't preserve a spark to re-ignite society. It was imperative that the flames of chaos not consume the people and knowledge it would take to start over. In that case, over time they would drift down anarchy. Accepting defeat went against everything Dave believed in and thought was good and noble about humans as a race.

Good people fight against things that are bad. They are builders and are at their best when working as a team over miles and generations to create something bigger, better, and more noble than any one man could do on his own.

Humans are at their worst when they tear things apart. When they can't work together or have discourse over miles, generations, and philosophies, then they are at the beginning of an end.

General Douglas MacArthur warned of this when he said, "*I am concerned for the security of our great nation; not so much because of any threat from without, but because of the insidious forces working from within.*"

LIZ

Liz was now on her sixth day feeling like a captive in her own suite. Until now, they'd been able to go down to the hotel restaurant for sandwiches and soup while Liz stayed in the penthouse with a guard. With her notoriety, joining would have been too big of a risk.

A few hotel employees were still coming to work and making what food they could, doling out toiletries and other supplies from the hotel's dwindling stock. The people who showed up for work dropped dramatically each day.

Junior volunteered to accompany a local security person from the hotel and one of the young men from the concierge staff into the city to scout for supplies and food they could store in the apartment. A few hours later, Junior returned alone with a nasty knife wound in his side. He related the story while Frank worked on his wound.

When they got down to the street level, it was clear there had been looting and a lot of damage. The streets were eerie and quiet. It felt wrong at a visceral level for such a huge, vibrant city to be so quiet. Even so, the security guard who'd lived there all of his life was sure there must be some stores behind iron shutters who would be willing to do business for cash. During their search, they'd been spotted by a large group of people who were clearly roaming the streets and preying on people like a pack of coyotes.

"The weirdness didn't stop there," Junior told them. "These weren't only the local hoodlums. We expected to see gangs and people being held up. This was different because there were women and children with them. Some of the people were dressed as if they were nine to five workers only a few days ago. Now they're like jackals preying on each other! When they came at us, the kid from the hotel staff took off. The security guard tried to reason with the gang. He said we'd trade with them and had some good stuff. The plan was to bargain from a position of strength and show we were armed. We wanted the gang to decide that trading would cost less lives than fighting. It was no use. They were a mob and acted like they didn't even speak English. The security guard got too close, and they attacked him. It took me a minute to clear them, because I was afraid of shooting him by accident."

Junior took a shaky breath and ran his hand across his eyes. "I fired off a few rounds, and most of them ran off. By the time I got to him, he was dead. They caved his head in. Even though I knew it was no use, I checked his pulse, and that's when I felt the knife go in my side. I was able to twist away and shoot the one with the knife, but there wasn't anything else I could do. I got back here as fast as I could, working my way past more gangs like the one we encountered. It's chaos and screams and sirens out there."

"Sirens are good," Frank said. "It means some of the police are still trying to settle things down."

The next morning, they made a trip downstairs for more supplies. When they returned, Frank was extremely agitated, and Junior was bleeding again. Jennifer wasn't with them. Frank's agitation was completely out of character, and Jennifer's absence was a terrible sign.

"She wandered over to another side of the room, and we lost track of her. We weren't worried because there were other guests in the area and it was safe enough before. I was sure it was okay because we were all in the lobby area." Frank slammed his fist into his palm. "I'm an idiot! I let my guard down." Frank spoke under his breath, eyes focused out the window. It was clear he wanted revenge but knew his place was here with Liz.

Junior picked up where Frank left off. "One of the busboys let some friends come in the back way for food. They were drunk or high, and within seconds most of the guests cleared out. We were headed back upstairs when we noticed Jennifer wasn't with us. Frank went back for her and found that some of them had pulled her into a side room and attacked her."

Frank resumed his account in a calmer, after action report manner. "I engaged two of the attackers and was able to put them down. Meanwhile, Junior knocked two men off of Jennifer and was helping her gather her clothes. The men Junior thought he'd chased off had only made a tactical retreat. They returned while he was helping Jennifer and stabbed him in the shoulder from behind. It was that damn busboy who did it! I'm sorry for saying it that bluntly, ma'am, but you need to know how it is out there."

"I should have never turned my back on him," Junior said.

"Jennifer tried to help Junior," Frank said. "She pushed them off him, and they cut her throat."

Junior's voice betrayed the anguish of losing the life of a young lady he was charged with protecting. "I tried to apply pressure until we could administer first aid. It was obvious she was gone and things were rapidly getting worse down there."

"We didn't know if they were coming back with five more thugs or fifty," Frank said. "I wanted to take them out, but I couldn't get a clear shot."

"We tried to find the hotel security," Carol sobbed, nearly hysterical. "There were so few security people to begin with. When Jennifer was killed, that was the last straw for whatever was holding this place together. They ran away."

"We couldn't find or flag down any police either," Frank added.

Liz insisted that they call a meeting of a few other people still staying at the top of the hotel. They could meet in her penthouse. It took less than thirty minutes to get everyone together, where they huddled in the penthouse to plan next steps. There were a few members of the film crew that were staying in other rooms as well as the male lead from the miniseries. They pooled their resources to stay in the penthouse. For now, the goal was just to be safe. No one had a plan yet for next steps.

The stone balconies off the penthouse were a common gathering spot for many of the people where, like Nero, they watched the city burn beneath them. It was hard to see details that far down. From what they could discern, the police were in running skirmishes with looters and rioters. As soon as it was put down in one area, it would flare up in another. Bottles would be thrown, shots fired, and people would scream and run. Then it would all become eerily silent for a while until a very similar scene would play out again on another street with another group. There didn't appear to be a rhyme or reason to the violence, and no ground was taken.

They had all thought of the hotel as a safe zone. Losing Jennifer proved how vulnerable they were.

Part Twelve

STRIFE

"Never lose hope. Storms make people stronger and never last forever."

- Roy T. Bennett

Waldorf Astoria, Chicago, IL

Jorge settled his two children into a hotel room in the corner of the third floor at the Waldorf. He'd been a doorman at the hotel for almost four years. When things went crazy, he decided to stay home and weather the storm. He had been used to chaos in his native Guatemala. The scale of this was so much larger than anything he experienced back there.

He and his family had been hunkered down in their small apartment, hiding from the sounds of riots and shots, when two men kicked in their door. Despite the chain and deadbolt, the frame gave way. While Jorge fought with one, his beloved Delmy fought like a wildcat to protect the children. Jorge plunged a large kitchen knife into his attacker, then he turned his head to find his wife's neck twisted to an unnatural angle. A tremendous fury overtook him, and he killed her attacker as well.

With no place else to go and the hope that criminals would never take time to search all the rooms in the hotel, he snuck in his children and what little food they had left. Occasionally, he could hear the guests in the halls or congregating downstairs. He dared not leave his children to investigate.

VINCE

Vince was watching the news of the riots and unrest in Chicago.

It reminded him of the news feeds of the war-torn eastern European countries. He had been trying all day and was nearly frantic by the time he finally got through to Ellie. Although Ellie said things were okay and tried to project calm, it was clear she was worried and scared. It was obvious to Vince if for no other reason than the fact she stayed on the phone with him so long. As much as he wanted to talk to Kate, he was enjoying talking to Ellie. He was worried they would lose the connection at any moment. This was the first time he had gotten through in days.

Ellie told him how great Malcolm was doing during the crisis stocking up on food and organizing the other men from the block to barricade the street with old cars at both ends of the block. They'd formed a neighborhood watch. So far, most of the crime, thugs, and looters had stayed away. Ellie wasn't sure how long they could hold out. She wondered rhetorically to Vince how long the current crisis would last.

"I arranged to get you a SAT phone from Uncle Dave's sources in the area," Vince told her. "We're still working out exactly how to get it to you. I promise I'll be there to help. I have some plans in the works."

"How can you get a phone delivered to me? It's not like Amazon is delivering right now," Ellie asked in amazement.

"Uncle Dave has offices in Chicago that procure government contracts for roads and bridges. Their building is about halfway between your place and downtown Chicago. He said they have several SAT phones at the office for their visits to more obscure locations, and they have drones they use for survey work. Those employees are bugging out with their families, and Uncle Dave convinced them to strap a SAT phone to a drone and get it to you. They're good men who are very loyal to Uncle Dave. They're also going to get another phone to some Hollywood starlet Uncle Dave knows who is trapped downtown, although no one has been able to get in touch with her and let her know it's coming. We can only hope she's still where they think. The last we heard, she was trapped at a luxury hotel before things got bad. I don't know when or how they'll get the drone to your house, but they have your address, so keep an eye out."

Ellie was so drained emotionally at this point all she had in response was a simple "Thank you."

More than two weeks into the unrest, things weren't getting better. While it appeared better in Louisville, Vince was sure it was only a temporary respite. The problem had spread all over the country. Things had come to such a boiling point in most major cities that issues in one area ignited chaos in other areas. Like organ failure in a body, the effect was cascading from city to city, and the leaders were hard pressed to stop it. By and large, the rural areas were spared the worst of it. Vince's concern and total focus was Chicago.

He talked to Ellie and Kate as often as possible. Frequently, he would get the "all circuits are busy" recording. That message made him so frustrated and furious he wanted to hit something. Vince also talked to Malcolm a time or two in order to understand his view of things in the neighborhood. It was his hometown, and Vince needed to know what he was seeing. Malcolm was becoming more worried as time passed and things didn't improve. However, he still held out hope the government would get things back under control soon.

Malcolm's neighborhood group had shot at two looters, leaving a heavy blood trail from one home leading out of the neighborhood. No one wanted to venture outside the block to see if they killed the looter. They hadn't been able to get any police response to their neighborhood before they armed themselves and barricaded the block. After the shooting, they still couldn't get any fire, police, or EMS response to take their reports.

Power had been out more often than not for about a week now. They were using the barbecue grill to heat food. They'd eaten the most perishable food first. They still had some of the food Malcolm had gotten from the bodega. Most families on the block were not as well supplied. Malcolm was alternating the generator he'd salvaged from the refrigerator to the freezer in the basement to keep his food supply fresh. Most people in the neighborhood shared because the perishable food would go bad soon. Malcolm told Vince that he expected the sharing to end when that food got lower. He didn't blame his neighbors and admitted he was holding back some of his own food as well. He'd asked Ellie and Kate to begin rationing the food he'd acquired and locate any container they could find to fill with water in addition to filling the bathtubs to the top while the taps were still running. The last couple of days, the water pressure had been dropping. They could still get water, but it was coming out at a trickle.

Vince decided he couldn't wait any longer. It would take a few days to get there by ground. If he waited any longer, he could be too late, and the consequences were too horrific to contemplate. If he was moving too fast, the worst would be wasted time and resources.

His first call after coming to that conclusion was to Uncle Dave to ask him to arrange the helicopter to French Lick. From there, he would pick up ground transportation. He didn't want to take the extra security men because he wasn't sure the trip was needed, and he didn't want other people risking their lives on his personal mission.

"It's better to be safe than sorry. Take the extra men," Uncle Dave reasoned. *"This could serve as a perfect training exercise in the event we need to rescue someone else."*

As a former Special Forces soldier, Vince knew well the value of training.

Dave told him they might have additional passengers coming along, sharing information on the plight of Liz Pendleton and her group in downtown Chicago. He wasn't sure if they needed out for sure, when, or how they would do it. He told Vince he would get him more information when he knew the details.

Vince didn't want to be distracted with some high maintenance Hollywood starlet and her friends. This trip was solely to rescue his girls. Still, he owed much of the tools, equipment, and options to help his girls to his uncle. Vince loved and respected Dave, and if he wanted Vince to bring a passenger or two back with them, he would.

They arranged for two security men to go with him. He thought he might need at least three vehicles to get all the passengers home if it went that far. Because he didn't want to take that many men along, he settled on two vehicles.

DAVE

Louis was tasked with the full-time job today of contacting people who needed to make it to the Colorado location. It was like a military operation calling everyone back to base.

No matter how busy he was with this work, his mind kept going back to Liz Pendleton. That girl had spunk. He couldn't help but like her. She was trapped in downtown Chicago, and they were all worried about her. Thankfully, she had her own security team.

When Vince called Dave, concerned about Ellie and Kate, Louis had been in the room and heard the angst in his voice. Dave told Louis later how he was able to make plans to get them a way to communicate, and he planned to use the same method for Liz. He asked Louis to keep calling and texting Liz's cell phone. So far, it was to no avail.

Dave gave instructions to the men in Chicago to accelerate the plan to pilot the drone with a SAT phone strapped underneath to her location. It had the range, but they had never flown it that high. Liz was on the fifty-second floor of the Waldorf Astoria in a penthouse condo. If she was still there, and if they could get the drone to her, they should be able to land it on the patio of the high-rise building with a note saying who it was from.

Dave knew the men were in a rush to get out of Chicago themselves. It was a testament to their loyalty that they offered to stay and do this.

If Vince was going in to Chicago and things were as bad as they were hearing, then those ladies needed a way to call out and help direct their rescue.

LIZ

It was nearing the end of the second week locked in the hotel.

The power was now out almost all the time. The gothic-style penthouse condo at the top of the hotel had huge balconies and plenty of light coming in from the skylights as well. They were able to warm up food in the fireplace as well as cook over the fire pit on the balcony.

The place was so crowded that Liz and Carol were sharing her room. Frank and Junior were in another room next door. Junior was still weak and sore from two knife wounds yet was determined to pull his own weight. It didn't help that Frank teased him about being slow to dodge and easy to cut. Frank was ex-Army and Junior a former Marine, and most of the banter centered on that fact. Although Liz didn't get it, she was happy to see the men in good spirits despite all they went through downstairs.

Steve Denver was the male lead on the miniseries with Liz. He and his security guard and a couple of other men that worked on the show moved from their rooms and were camping out in the main room of the Penthouse on couches. Steve was older than Liz and full of himself. He'd made a few halfhearted attempts to share her room. She would have been repulsed if his attempts hadn't been so weak and humorous. She felt sorry for him at first, then he decided he should take charge and organize the group and their defenses. Liz made sure Steve knew he was a guest and his input would not be needed. She hated to emasculate him like that in front of the others, but she couldn't have the group divided right now. To his credit, Steve did stay quiet after that even though he may have been a bit sullen. That was preferable to meddling and flirting.

Frank once again made the long trek down the stairs to scavenge for food. He reported back that very few of the staff had showed up for work and much of the food had already been looted. All that remained were things like rice and peanut butter, which ironically was exactly what they needed. He was able to bring those back as well as some tuna, salami, and a few other odds and ends he found ignored in a back corner of the food storage area. He hid what he couldn't carry to be retrieved later. While they weren't eating like kings, they weren't starving either. Those foods had a long shelf life and a lot of the nutrients a body needed. They were also portable if they needed to leave the hotel.

Frank's comment about possibly leaving worried Liz. She'd had the same thought herself but had been afraid to voice it. After Frank spoke the words, it had to be considered.

He reported seeing a few people from the staff blockading doors. One of them told Frank a police squad car would roll by once a day or so. As soon as the police were gone, the thugs would come back. The police were using the hotel as more of a place to stop and rest up than to establish order. It was good news that the police were still fighting; it was bad news that they appeared to be losing. Everyone in the city was so weary.

"I suspect the only reason these last hotel employees are protecting the place or holding the door is because a few of them have brought their own families here and hidden them a few floors up in rooms," Frank postulated. "The police I did see remind me of a teacher trying to keep order in one of those crowded inner city schools. They were going through the motions because they were expected to, but the air of defeat was evident in their eyes and body language. How long before they quit trying altogether?"

Outside on the streets, it was much worse. Liz and her team began to discuss what to do if things didn't come back to order soon. The food was running low and would soon run out. Eventually a gang of thugs would come up here seeking valuables. Or when food or water ran out, hunger would force their group out into the street. Neither option was good. As a group, they decided to stay put for the time being. No one truly wanted to venture out at this time anyway.

Liz had a sinking feeling they were living on borrowed time and had only delayed making a hard decision. For now, it was easier to sit tight and hope for rescue. There was enough food for now as long as they rationed it. Many of them still believed order would be restored soon. In a worst case scenario, perhaps the gangs and looters would lose some of their steam and move on, or even kill enough of each other off to make things safer. Liz spent a great deal of time contemplating possible courses of action. She liked to sit on the balcony close to the fire pit. They were feeding it from pieces of furniture salvaged from rooms below. Liz grew accustomed to the sounds below, ranging from long periods of eerie silence to gunshots, screams, and sirens.

It was another sound that shook her mind from her melancholy mood and put her senses on alert. A faint buzz. Searching for the source of the sound, she saw what appeared to be a bird headed directly for her balcony. It didn't take Liz long to discern that it wasn't a bird, it was manmade.

She ran to the glass.

"Frank!" she cried.

Frank came out, gun drawn, ready for combat right as the drone landed. He waited a moment and then approached the drone cautiously. He pulled a heavily taped note off the drone and used his knife to slit it open from the bottom. He held the note and envelope to the light and peered inside, examined the note more closely, and read it briefly. He turned to Liz and deadpanned, "It's for you."

While she was reading the note, Frank asked, "Do you know Dave Cavanaugh?"

"Yes, I do."

"There's a phone in a container strapped to the underside of the drone." Frank handed it to Liz.

As soon as she powered it up, the phone rang. Liz was so startled she almost dropped it. It was Dave on the other end with his lovely western cultured voice.

"How is Chicago this time of year?" Liz could only laugh in reply.

Her laughter and tears of relief changed the mood of the group immediately. While they weren't saved, they did finally have contact with the outside world.

When she got control of herself, Liz filled Dave in on the conditions in Chicago.

Dave apologetically informed her, *"I can't get air transport in to get you and your team out. However, if things don't improve soon I do have some other plans in the works."*

"What do you mean?" Liz asked.

"I can't go into too much detail right now other than to let you know that I have some plans to get a team into the city via land. There is another family a few miles away that may need help getting out of the city as well. I need you and your team to think about a plan to make it a few miles away to an extraction point. I will try to get a team to the hotel. If that can't be done, can your group make it a few miles? If we can pull it off and send a team in, you need to be ready to go with either plan at a moment's notice."

"Thank you. We'll discuss the options and make plans," Liz said. "I will keep in touch hourly. I'd rather have you and your people provide direction and advice."

Dave sighed on the other end of the phone. *"The SAT phone signal isn't reliable.*

We need to minimize contact and be prepared to be very concise on calls. You should assume each time we speak that we will not be able to connect again."

"Why?" Liz asked, confused.

"The SAT phone system is either having technical issues or being purposefully sabotaged. Sometimes it takes hours or days to get a call through. Liz, you should know that strong, resilient people survive chaotic situations at a much higher rate than weaker people. If you expect little or no help, you will be stronger and more likely to survive this. If I direct a plan and it suddenly becomes untenable, it could be worse for you if you expect to be saved. You're a survivor, and you have good people with you."

When Liz remained silent, and Dave worried she was afraid, he said in his most fatherly voice, *"Liz, don't think that doesn't mean I won't move Heaven and Earth to try and help you any way I can. I'm here for you. Twenty minutes ago, you didn't expect to be talking to me now, so things are already looking up. Stay positive. You're a natural leader, whether you know it or not. If you want those people to survive and feel more powerful than they are, make them feel positive, empowered, and optimistic. I know you can do it."*

Part Thirteen

FRIENDS

"Let me not pray to be sheltered from dangers, but to be fearless in facing them. Let me not beg for the stilling of my pain, but for the heart to conquer it."

- Rabindranath Tagore

VINCE

The helicopter touched down in a field near French Lick, Indiana. Vince was accompanied by Andy and Dwight, two Special Forces operators. They had been assigned to the Carrollton location after getting some cursory training in Colorado. Vince would have preferred to work alone. He didn't want to be responsible for them. However, the practical part of his mind knew he needed them. If he was going to bring a handful of people out of Chicago, through a couple of hundred miles of highway and small towns, their experience and firepower would be a welcome addition.

Andy was a big, blond-haired man who had been a Ranger in both Iraq and Afghanistan. It helped the team comradery that Andy was happy and good natured. That was always preferable in a tight-knit team because it helped people relax and increased camaraderie.

Dwight was harder to figure out. He shared enough of his Special Forces background that confirmed he was imminently qualified. He also spent a good deal of time with a Blackwater-type private contracting firm after he left active duty. That stint was a double-edged sword for Vince. Although they hired and trained the best, it worried him that some of the men didn't take as much of a moral high ground as Vince and his uncle mandated. Dwight admitted there was a lot he wanted to leave behind, and he wanted to get back close to home in Indiana. Vince chose to take him at this word the same as his uncle had done. Dwight was tall and dark haired, broad of shoulder and lean at the waist. He moved silently, with a spooky economy of motion that could sneak right up on you.

When they stepped off the helicopter at French Lick, they were near a massive country junkyard with a few metal pole barns scattered around, which presumably acted as shops for the work or as storage. From the outside looking in, it was a mess of rust and destruction holding nothing of value. A grizzled older man came out of one of the barns with a shotgun in one hand and a yellow Motorola walkie talkie clipped on the breast pocket of his Carhartt jacket. Gus and Vince had talked before the flight, so Gus knew he was coming and why; he was just being cantankerous and cautious. Vince stepped forward with his hands palms out and identified himself. Although they'd spoken, Gus hadn't yet met him face to face. Still a bit wary, Gus asked how Dave and his wife were doing.

"Dave has been a widow for most of his adult life. He lost his wife Tess to a drunk driver back in the seventies," Vince answered.

This mollified Gus. He lowered his shotgun and spoke into the walkie. "Everything seems all right here. Although to be on the safe side, sit tight, stay ready, and watch the perimeter."

Gus led them into a modest brick home at the edge of the junkyard and offered them drinks. When they were seated at the kitchen table, Vince talked more at length about what he needed. He hadn't said as much as he would have liked on the phone earlier.

"I have the things you need," Gus told him. "I owe Dave a lot. I'm still not one hundred percent sure why I should trust you yet, though."

Vince tried hard to hide his impatience. He was in a hurry to get to Chicago. He dialed Dave's private SAT phone number and handed the phone to Gus. He could hear Gus's half of the conversation as he paced the room. Dave was inviting Gus and his family to move to Chartertown Kentucky, at least temporarily.

"Thank you for the offer," Gus said into the phone. "For now, we're fine, and I have plans to make this place much safer than your little town in Kentucky. You and your family have a safe shelter here whenever you needed it."

They both chuckled, and Vince got a better idea of the cantankerous old man and how he operated. Some people just had a different way about them. When Gus hung up with Dave, Vince handed him a solar charger for the SAT phone and told him to keep it close.

The place didn't appear worth much and definitely wasn't worth attacking *or* defending from Vince's viewpoint. Later, when Gus took him on a short tour, he could see it was a labyrinth of junk. Amongst the maze of cars Gus had stored food, garden plots, and fallback positions. Although it piqued Vince's curiosity, he was anxious to get on his way. Vince and Gus agreed they could do some trading down the road. Chartertown Carrollton and Gus each had things the other would need.

Gus led them to another pole barn to a pair of 4X4s he just finished modifying for the trip to Chicago, then spoke into the walkie talkie to his sons, telling them to come on out and meet some friends.

ELLIE

As much as she hated to admit it, she needed Vince.

It would have been easy to swallow her pride if it was only her and Kate. This would be hard on Malcolm; he was a proud man, and Chicago was his hometown. They lived only a few blocks from the auto repair shop his dad ran for forty-five years and only a few miles from the company where Malcolm was an HR director.

Ellie was proud of Malcolm. He had created a safe zone in the middle of the chaos of Chicago for the time being. It couldn't hold if things didn't get better soon. Each day she prayed to see the police or the National Guard show up announcing the nightmare was over. Food and water were running lower and the gangs and looters were running out of lower-hanging fruit to prey on. They would soon turn their attention to more protected targets like their block.

It was concerning that before they put up the roadblock even people Malcolm had known for years were acting strangely. They would visit to make small talk when they hadn't before, looking past him or over his shoulder. Malcolm couldn't decide if he was being paranoid or if they were trying to determine how well stocked up they were. He suggested to his neighbors that they board up all the doors and windows on the backs of their houses and to barricade the narrow access lanes between the homes. He insisted they keep the roadblocks on each end of the street manned twenty-four hours a day, seven days a week.

So far, Malcolm's plans were working. The people on the block took comfort in a level of refuge many places in the city didn't have. Confidence and hope were slowly creeping back in. Some of the people were even discussing a community garden and homeschooling sessions for the children if the situation lasted much longer.

Ellie was worried that the looters were only going after other targets for now in deference to Malcolm's defenses. When the gangs got hungrier for food and power, these defenses wouldn't be enough. The previous night one of the more violent local gangs came to the roadblock demanding access, saying the street was city property. Had Malcolm been at the roadblock, he could have avoided the ensuing bloodshed. Once they showed weakness or gave in, the demands would not stop. The leader was a local hoodlum and drug dealer named Raheem Jackson. Raheem was as bad of a thug as any of them. Malcolm knew him since he'd been a kid and had swept up around the shop and done odd jobs when Malcolm's father was still alive.

Raheem was mean, but he was also smart and calculating. Malcolm thought he could reason with him. It was Raheem's kid brother Malik who was the real unstable one. Malik was rumored to be involved with some heinous crimes. Raheem planned things for the gang that kept the cash coming in and relatively few of them in jail. Malik was the crazy one in the family. He had a bit of a *Scarface* mindset. If any in the gang had been old enough to know the movie, they would have noticed some very similar mannerisms. With a huge scar running from his right eye to the back of his lower jaw and an eye that drooped a bit, Malik was easy to pick out in a crowd. The rumor was that it was due to a fight with another kid while in juvie. Malik was the only one still alive after the fight. He'd been a minor at the time, and the horrendous gash on his face assured him of a successful self-defense plea. That and the fact that no one since then had been willing to testify against him was why he was free today after a stay in a psychiatric facility.

At the blockade, an argument ensued between some men from the block and some of Raheem's men. Words turned into yells and yells into a fight. One of the neighbors was stabbed, and from reports, it sounded like Malik was the assailant. Arriving at the end of the melee, Malcom couldn't save Mr. Stevens, but he was able to ensure that one of the gang members took some number six shot with him from his dad's old shotgun as he left. The amount of blood he trailed proved he was hit hard and might not make it. Malcolm was relatively certain Raheem had taken some of the stray pellets as well. Although Raheem didn't appear too much worse for the wear, that surely ended any chance at negotiation with them.

Mr. Stevens probably wouldn't make it to the next day, either. If he didn't, they would have to bury him with the other two neighbors in the front yard of the vacant house on the corner. The graveyard that was a temporary solution a week ago suddenly had a more permanent appearance, which was both scary and depressing.

After things settled down, Malcolm went home to let Ellie know he was okay and the neighborhood was safe for the moment. About that time, Ellie got a call from Vince announcing he was on his way to get them out. Her sigh of relief was more audible than she would have liked for Malcolm to hear.

"It might take a couple of days," Vince told her, *"but I can be reached on this SAT phone number if you need me. On another note, there's a VIP trapped in downtown Chicago that may come in on foot if you're okay with taking in a boarder or two? It's a favor to Uncle Dave."*

"Um...okay," Ellie agreed.

"It's a woman, Liz Pendleton, and a couple of her friends."

"Liz Pendleton!" Ellie exclaimed. "Kate will be so excited to meet her. Malcolm probably will as well."

It would definitely cause a stir on the block.

LIZ

Liz decided it was time to get out of Chicago.

It wasn't a unanimous decision. Steve Denver and some of the film crew folks were too scared to leave the hotel. They didn't think they could make a long walk or survive in the streets below. Just getting up and down the stairs from the penthouse to the ground level was an arduous task that took them hours and several breaks in the stairwell.

Their food supply was low, and they'd heard screams actually inside the hotel not far from Liz's penthouse. When the security team ventured into the halls and stairwells they heard shooting in the hotel below, they could see smoke and hear shooting on the streets from Liz's balcony. What finally convinced her it was time to go was the fact that among all the chaos, she hadn't heard a police or ambulance siren in three days. It would be a long time before the city recovered. It may never be the same.

The assembled people were divided into two groups. One would bunker into the condo and try to scavenge food when it was safe. Liz, her assistant Carol, Frank, and Junior would try to make it on foot to a private home eight miles away that Dave told her about via one of their rare phone calls. Dave didn't think they could get a car downtown right now and told her it was her choice to try and make the eight-mile trek. He understood if she wanted to wait for another option.

Liz chose to take the risk. Although she didn't try to talk anyone else into going with her, she was glad when Frank and Junior agreed to go. This was well beyond anything they'd signed up for. She was afraid for Carol and wasn't convinced she could make it. At the same time, she didn't believe Carol would be any safer staying behind. Eight miles would have been a short run that she could do in a couple of hours under normal circumstances. Under the current conditions, both Frank and Junior told her that twelve hours would be more likely, assuming all went well, which by the look on their faces they were far from sure it would.

They planned to rest well today and pack the most comfortable clothing they had and add some food and essentials. Frank went through her backpack after it was packed the same as if she was a kid going to camp. *Camp Death* was the thought that went through her mind as she watched him. She didn't know whether to laugh or cry at those thoughts, she only knew in her heart it was the right thing to do.

The plan was to leave at three in the morning, the idea being to get much of the trip done in the wee hours of the morning, when the criminal element was most likely to be sleeping off the alcohol or drugs that most often accompanied their rampages. With luck, they would make it to the address Dave had given her before the goons woke up.

As Liz was preparing to leave the hotel she contacted the woman Dave Cavanaugh had told her about. It took several calls over three hours to get through the electronic congestion. She weighed delaying the trek by a day to ensure she could get through on the phone. She needed to know there was a safe place to go at the end of this trip.

When Ellie Weathers answered on the first ring of perhaps the thirtieth attempt at calling, Liz's relief was audible. She spoke with Ellie, relieved at the offer to open up her home to Liz and her friends.

"Thank you for allowing us to come to your home," Liz said. "The plan is to leave in the middle of the night and travel through the early morning hours. I don't know when we'll get there, but we don't want to be mistaken as intruders when we arrive."

At two-thirty in the morning, Frank woke the people who were going. Liz and her team had prepared the night before and left quietly. Frank took point; Liz and Carol were in the middle, with Junior bringing up the rear. Fifty-two flights of stairs were terrible on their legs, but most of them already had experience with it and knew how to pace themselves. Despite that, they stopped several times to work out cramps in their calves. They did run into a few people in the stairwell of the hotel. Most were either sleeping off a drunk or not interested in dealing with two well-armed men.

When they stepped out onto the street, the smell of smoke, oil, and something that smelled like burnt tar pervaded the air. Wailing and crying could be heard in the distance. Liz thought this must be what the aftermath of battle was like.

They traveled the first few blocks without incident, stopping occasionally in an alley or behind a dumpster to recheck the map with a Magritte tactical flashlight that both men carried. Sometime after four in the morning, they ducked into an alley to check their location against the map and accidently woke a man sitting on a chair under a blanket. When he stood, it was obvious he was armed. It was when he took in a deep breath to yell for others that Frank had no choice but to silence him with a knife.

Liz heard enough screams and shooting from the balcony that she expected violence and thought she was prepared for it. Seeing death up close and personal wasn't like in the movies or in a book. It was sad, dirty, messy and so wasteful, a man's life gone for no reason other than bad luck and bad decisions. Her mind was spinning with a million questions, and her stomach was turning. What if the man meant them no harm? Did he have children? Was he married? Perhaps he was only hungry. Maybe they just surprised him.

All these thoughts only took a couple of seconds, the time it took for Frank to ease the man's body to the ground. Even as those thoughts crossed her mind, Liz knew she was wrong and Frank had done what he must. It didn't make it easier. A man was dead and her team killed him. When Carol's shock wore off and she locked eyes with the empty, unblinking eyes of the dead man, she screamed. The stealth of the kill was undone.

Other men and half-naked women came pouring out of the building. Frank, Junior, Carol, and Liz took off running. The crowd gave chase. Normally Junior could have outrun them all, but he was injured. Liz was fast under normal circumstances. Under these circumstances, she was afraid of losing her footing. A fall could be fatal. Carol was in full panic mode, and they fought to keep her with the group. Frank was the calmest, purposefully staying at the rear to cover them from the gunfire of the pursuing horde.

Acting as the rear guard, he took two hits, one in the back of the thigh and another through and through on his lower right chest. Both Junior and Frank returned fire, rapidly changing magazines. Fortunately, the punks with guns were just as surprised as they were and hesitated.

They stopped behind a dumpster to tend Frank's wounds and be ready to return fire again if needed. Liz assumed the bullet pierced Frank's lung when she saw the bubbled blood on his mouth. She had no idea how bad a lung wound was or if Frank could recover from it. She was sure he needed medical attention and also sure he would not get it here. Frank spat the blood into his hand, peering at the bubbles for a long moment.

He looked into Liz's eyes. "I'm so sorry I couldn't finish this job. I never expected to like one of you Hollywood types, but I did."

"Don't try to talk," Liz said.

"I've got about five minutes left on this Earth, Liz, fifteen at best. Maybe I'd live if I was in an operating room, but I ain't and won't be." Frank coughed up more blood.

"Save your strength, Frank. I'll find you an ambulance if I have to steal one," Junior implored, tears on his face.

Frank shook his head. "Grant me one favor, Junior. Make my last mission a successful one," he whispered, focusing directly on Junior. The blood bubbles were getting slower. "Hand me my gun. You all need to haul ass and make it out of here alive. Don't waste my death by standing here talking till I die."

There wasn't a dry eye in the group as they left. Although he was young, Junior had seen a lot of death. Brokenhearted and teary eyed, he ran through the night. Tonight, he was much older than his years.

Not long after they left, they could hear the distinctive sound of the .45 caliber 1911 pistol barking behind them. Frank had cleared their back trail. They needed to focus on the path ahead.

As the day was breaking, they were concerned with being spotted. They were only about a mile from their destination, which equated to about six blocks in Chicago terrain. While they were searching for a spot to rest, they were hailed from a window by a woman who was likely on drugs. The yells caught the attention of a ragged man and woman begging on the street. Carol tried to give them some food as the group walked past and was stabbed in the thigh with a broken bottle for her generosity. Junior grabbed the man who stabbed Carol from behind in a chokehold. People were screaming, and they needed to move on. Liz turned her head for only a moment, and when she looked back, Junior had plunged his battle-worn black Ka-bar knife between the man's ribs.

The momentary pause was broken when the woman ran off screaming at the top of her lungs, "They have food!" Other ragged figures came out of the woodwork, headed for them. Liz took charge, and they ran. They made several zigs and zags through the buildings in an attempt to lose their pursuers. Carol was sobbing and needed help from both Junior and Liz. At least she didn't give up.

They soon found themselves on a block with a few looted businesses and more that appeared to have been boarded up for quite some time. They made it into the back of a store that sold clothing and shoes. They did their best to clean and bandage Carol's wound. Liz didn't think they could make it much further in the daylight with Junior distracted by having to help carry Carol. They needed to rest, and Liz insisted they take a breather and try again later.

Liz's rest was filled with indecision. She didn't know what to do. She decided to keep trying to call Ellie until she could get through. She needed someone to talk to and some advice. She finally got through and spoke to Ellie.

"My husband knows the area well and thinks it's too many blocks to make it through gangs and looters in the daylight. Laying low for the time being is a good idea. He may have another idea also." Ellie passed the phone to Malcolm.

After listening to Liz describe what she knew of her surroundings, he asked her to peek out the front of the window and find a building with a faded sign reading WEATHERS AUTO REPAIR. Liz did; it was only a few buildings down.

"Go to the side alley. There's a back door to the auto repair building. It was my father's. I own it now. I'll give you the code to the mechanical lock on the back door. I'll come get you. It will be a few hours before I can get there, though. Watch for a red minivan. I need you all to be ready. Don't waste any time getting in the van, though, because the junkies and gangsters will come running when they see me."

"We'll be ready. How will we know when you're coming?"

"You may not. If we can't get a call through, I don't want to honk. Keep an eye out for the van. I can't leave it to come looking for you, so you all need to be alert and ready."